"What time s
for dinner?"

Rob grinned at [barcode: ID661548]
her. She was standing in front of her desk,
her arms crossed over her chest.

"When hell freezes over," she snapped.

"Now, Sabrina," Rob whispered in her
ear, "what is it about me that you find
so annoying?"

Sabrina sighed and threw up her hands in
defeat. "I want to know how we met," she
said in a decisive tone, facing Rob. "I'm not
playing your stupid game any—"

The last word died in a strangled choke
when his mouth covered hers. The kiss
was only a brief one. Yet she was trembling
when he stepped back, her heart racing in
her chest.

"You're really enjoying this, aren't you?"
Sabrina almost growled at him.

"You bet," Rob said, laughing. "You've had
your own way for too long, Sabrina Marsh.
It's time someone challenged you a bit."

"Someone like you, I suppose?"

He reached out to touch her hand, sending
sparks of sensation all the way up her arm.
"Someone exactly like me."

Gina Wilkins has always thought that pilots make extremely romantic hero figures. And so they do, as you'll find out in her latest Harlequin Temptation novel, *A Perfect Stranger*. Living a quarter of a mile away from an air-force base, Gina is lucky to catch a glimpse of real, live, handsome pilots. Not that she should need to—after all, Gina has her own personal hero: her six-foot-four, blue-eyed husband, who happens to be a private pilot and, she adds, "looks wonderful in a flight jacket and aviator glasses...."

Books by Gina Wilkins

HARLEQUIN TEMPTATION
174–HERO IN DISGUISE
198–HERO FOR THE ASKING
204–HERO BY NATURE
212–CAUSE FOR CELEBRATION
245–A BRIGHT IDEA
262–A STROKE OF GENIUS
283–COULD IT BE MAGIC
299–CHANGING THE RULES
309–AFTER HOURS
337–A REBEL AT HEART

Don't miss any of our special offers. Write to us at the following address for information on our newest releases.

Harlequin Reader Service
P.O. Box 1397, Buffalo, NY 14240
Canadian address: P.O. Box 603,
Fort Erie, Ont. L2A 5X3

A Perfect Stranger
GINA WILKINS

Harlequin Books

TORONTO • NEW YORK • LONDON
AMSTERDAM • PARIS • SYDNEY • HAMBURG
STOCKHOLM • ATHENS • TOKYO • MILAN

In memory of Dave Grundfest, Jr.,
who lived his dream of flight
and encouraged me to pursue my own dreams
"Oh! I have slipped the surly bonds of earth . . .
Put out my hand, and touched the face of God."

Published July 1991

ISBN 0-373-25453-9

A PERFECT STRANGER

1

"EXCUSE ME, but haven't we met somewhere before?"

Oh, puh-leeze. Sabrina couldn't believe she'd heard the man correctly. Surely he hadn't really used that tired old pickup line. She turned her head to look at him coolly, aware that her strictly tailored navy suit and primly up-swept hair lent dignity to her appearance. "I beg your pardon?"

At her well-practiced, frosty tone, the man's cheeks darkened a bit, but he persisted. "You look very familiar. I feel as though we've met."

Shifting her briefcase to her other hand, Sabrina took a moment to give her elevator companion an unemotional, head-to-toe perusal. It wasn't an unpleasant task. He was certainly attractive in an athletic way. Tall, well built—dimples and blinding smile—blue eyes, black hair worn shorter than she might have expected considering his stylish clothing. No woman with normal vision, which Sabrina certainly had, or a normal hormone count, which she'd occasionally questioned during the past few years, could meet this man and then completely forget him. "I'm afraid you're mistaken."

And then with the air of someone unaccustomed to having her words questioned, she turned to the front of the elevator and watched the floor numbers light up as the car descended. She wasn't feeling guilty about leaving work an hour early, she told herself, the man already out of her mind. Dammit, she deserved an extra hour now and then, even though she was the boss. It really hadn't been necessary for her secretary to act as though Sabrina had grown an extra head just because she'd announced that she'd break away from the office a little earlier than usual on this lovely spring Tuesday afternoon. Couldn't Julia understand that even Sabrina occasionally felt the walls closing around her, suffocating her?

"I really wasn't trying anything funny," the man said, interrupting her thoughts again. His voice was just as friendly as it had been before her rebuff. Not a man who was easily discouraged, she thought before he caught her completely off-guard by explaining, "It's just that you remind me of someone I once knew. Her name was Sabrina Marsh."

The car bumped to a stop just as Sabrina turned quickly to face him. Stumbling, she put out a hand to steady herself against the cool metal wall at the same time as the man caught her shoulders. "Okay?" he asked, smiling down at her from his superior height. Being five-seven herself, she didn't often have to look quite so far upward.

She cleared her throat. "I'm Sabrina Marsh. But I—"

"Just a minute." Nodding an apology to the people trying to enter the elevator around them, he led Sabrina out of the way, keeping one hand on her shoulder. "Now," he said when they were standing in the lobby of the upscale office building, "we can talk."

Still adjusting to the fact that he'd known her name, she frowned as she again shifted the heavy briefcase. "I'm sorry, but if we've met, I've forgotten." Her hormone count must be in worse condition than she'd thought if she'd ever spent any time with this man and couldn't remember him, she mused ruefully.

"Rob Davis," he supplied helpfully, watching for her reaction.

The name was no more familiar than the face. "Rob Davis," she repeated, uncomfortable with the awkwardness of the exchange. She was a woman who made it a point to always be in control of any situation. Being out of control brought back those old feelings of ineptitude, of vulnerability. She didn't like being made to feel that way now.

"I'm—" No, she decided abruptly, she wouldn't apologize again. If the man had any courtesy at all, he'd end the suspense and just tell her who he was and how they'd met.

"I'm in a bit of a rush," she hinted broadly, glancing at her no-nonsense, precise-to-the-second watch. "Was there something you wanted?"

Undeterred by her brusqueness, he only continued to smile, making excellent use of the masculine dimples at the corners of his nicely shaped mouth. A man like this would probably be amazed that he'd escaped any woman's attention, she thought, but he hid it well if he was. "It's good to see you, Brie. How's Colin? And your mom, does she still make those wonderful apple-raisin pies?"

Exasperated, Sabrina resisted the impulse to drop her purse and briefcase and press both hands to her temples, where a dull headache threatened. The man—Rob Davis, she reminded herself—spoke with such confident familiarity, calling her by the nickname only family and close friends used, naming her brother, casually mentioning her mother's best-known dessert. "Colin's fine. My mother died several years ago. How—?"

His bright blue eyes turned warm with sympathy. He had a very expressive face. He'd obviously never bothered to learn to mask his emotions, as Sabrina had done years ago. "I'm sorry," he said and he sounded sincere. "She was a lovely woman. You must miss her very much."

Caught off-guard again, Sabrina answered huskily. "Yes. I do."

His smile returned, making her suspect it was never gone for long. "You're still not convinced we've ever met, are you?"

She answered with total honesty. "No. I'm not."

He affected a sigh, though amusement glinted in his eyes and deepened his voice. "I'm crushed."

It would take a lot more than that to crush this man. He was the embodiment of healthy male ego. The type of man Sabrina had long since learned to avoid. "I'm sorry, but you don't even look familiar to me. Are you a friend of Colin's?"

"Not exactly," he replied unhelpfully. His vivid blue eyes were decidedly mischievous when he asked her, "You honestly don't remember me at all?"

A frown creased her brow. Staring at him, Sabrina pursed her lips as she considered, then rejected, various ways she could have known him. Her family had traveled extensively during her youth. She'd met many people over the years, forgotten plenty of them. They'd spent some time in Texas during her childhood and she had liked that state more than any of the many others where she'd lived. She'd moved back to Dallas soon after her divorce several years ago. She would surely remember this man if she'd met him during the past few years. Wouldn't she?

His age was hard to guess. She was thirty-three; she assumed he was close to the same age, judging from the fine lines at the corners of his eyes and the air of utter, mature confidence. She wondered if they'd attended high school together the year she'd lived in Irving, Texas. But she didn't remember anyone named Rob Davis, or anyone who looked like this.

"No," she said finally and if she felt any regret, she was certain it didn't show in her voice. "I don't remember you. Who are you?"

He grinned. "I told you. I'm Rob Davis."

Annoyed, she turned. "I don't have time for this." And she started to walk away, half-convinced the man had some loose parts rattling around in that very attractive head.

"Wait." He fell quickly into step beside her as she headed for the doors. "Aren't you even interested in how we met?"

She didn't slow down. "Not enough to play these games to find out."

"Games can be fun at times," he suggested.

"Yes. For children."

"Come on, Brie, loosen up. Surely you haven't changed that much. You used to like to have fun."

She flicked him a glance. "I'm supposed to be having fun now?"

He grinned engagingly. "Call it a challenge. I'll give you three guesses about how we met. Name the stakes."

"Sorry. I don't play guessing games." Approaching the revolving door, she reached for it.

He caught her wrist. "What kind of games do you play?"

"I *don't*." She jerked her wrist out of his loose grasp. "Goodbye." And then she hurried through the door before he could reply.

He was right behind her when she stepped out onto the sidewalk. She was annoyed that it might take a policeman to rid her of her uninvited companion. He slid a pair of aviator-style glasses onto his nose to shield his eyes against the bright sunlight, then smiled down at her. She had the rather whimsical impression that his smile was even brighter than the sunlight. Pushy, but definitely gorgeous, she mused with a touch of wistfulness she refused to acknowledge.

"Have dinner with me," he said. It wasn't a question. More a demand, she decided irritably, wistfulness gone.

"Sorry." Head down, she turned quickly toward the parking lot, thinking of the security guard who'd be waiting there.

"We'll have seafood. You still love seafood, don't you? Fried shrimp, lobster, crab legs?"

How did he *know* these things? Looking wildly for Cal, the security guard, she gripped her purse more tightly and refused to answer.

"Brie—"

She turned then, furiously. "Stop calling me that! Either tell me who you are and how we met or get lost. I told you, I don't like playing games."

He looked at her for a long time and she thought that his expression looked oddly sad. "I think it's been much too long since you allowed yourself to play at all," he observed perceptibly. "What happened to you, Brie?"

That made her chin lift defensively. "I grew up," she answered, the words clipped. "The hard way. Now if you'll excuse me . . ."

"We really do know each other, you know," he said conversationally, his lazy smile returning.

"If that's true," she returned, her tone indicating she didn't really believe him, "then I must have blocked you from my mind because I didn't like you."

He didn't even wince. Instead, his smile broadened as he spread his arms in a playfully egotistic gesture. "Impossible. What's not to like?"

She bit hard on the inside of her lip to resist an unexpected urge to smile. *Don't encourage the man, Sabrina.* "I'm sure I could think of something," she murmured instead. Then, turning sharply on one high heel, she walked to her car, head up, never looking back.

He didn't follow her this time, though she knew he was still there as she climbed behind the wheel and drove out of the lot. Only then did she allow herself one last glance into the rearview mirror. Not bad at all, she thought regretfully, memorizing the sight of him in the bright afternoon sun, his dark hair tossed by a mischievous breeze as he stood with legs braced wide and hands on his slender hips. How sad that he was such a fruitcake.

She drove home with the car windows down, her radio tuned to a rock station. Again, guilt nagged at her, reminding her that the office was still open, her employees busily working while Sabrina enjoyed the weather. She shoved those thoughts away. Something about the crisp first-week-in-April air, the greening trees and blooming bushes along the roadside, the brilliant blue of the unclouded sky made her feel young and vibrantly alive. And then a tiny voice in her head asked if those feelings were at least partially due to a handsome man's bright smile, a spark of masculine appreciation in a pair of roguish blue eyes.

She sternly rejected the idea as soon as it occurred to her. She wasn't a schoolgirl panting for the campus jock—not anymore. She was a thirty-three-year-old divorced career woman with an active, if conservative social life. The men she dated were polite, usually quite a bit older than herself. None of them would have irritated her with that silly guessing game business.

Telling herself that she'd been attracted to him only because he was an unusually handsome man, that she'd almost been tempted to play along with his game only because it was hard for her to resist a challenge, she made an effort to put him out of her mind. An effort that failed miserably, she realized when she absently noted that the clear sky was the same color as Rob Davis's eyes.

Perhaps her life *had* become just a bit too predictable during the past few years. Maybe that explained this sudden fascination with an attractive, mysterious and decidedly odd stranger.

THE DUPLEX in which Sabrina lived was a two-story red brick building with freshly-painted white trim and shutters. She had purchased the building over three years earlier and had promptly rented the left half to a very nice couple, the O'Neals, who still lived there with their daughter, Mandy. Each side of the duplex contained a living room, kitchen and dining room downstairs and two bedrooms and a bath upstairs. Large windows and open layout made the snug apartments seem roomy and light. Sabrina loved her home. Maybe because it was the first one she could really call hers.

Before she could fit her key into her lock, the door vibrated with the weight of a heavy body hurled against it from the inside, accompanied by a series of frantic, welcoming barks. "All right, Angel, give me time to get inside," she called out in amusement.

Inside her living room, she reached down to hug the sleek Doberman pinscher who squirmed and wagged like a puppy in his owner's arms, his black body shining, brown ears pointed attentively, brown muzzle rubbing adoringly against her face. "You big marshmallow," Sabrina accused him fondly, though she knew her loving description was hardly apt. Angel might act like a sweet pet with his owner, but he was an expertly trained guard dog, fully capable of tearing out a throat if so ordered. He was much better protection for Sabrina's home than the expensive, heavy-duty locks she'd had installed on all the doors and windows.

Her apartment was furnished and decorated with the deliberate intent to provide a warm welcome when she came home. Choosing antiques and reproductions of nineteenth-century furnishings, she'd made liberal use of her favorite color—yellow—in combination with rose and teal, with touches of gleaming brass and lots of fresh flowers. Her bedroom followed the same theme.

Stripping out of her business suit, she slipped into a red satin kimono, a present from her brother Colin when he'd returned from a photo assignment in Japan. Unlike Sabrina, Colin had never minded living like a gypsy. He'd rented an apartment in Dallas a couple of years earlier, claiming to need a home base and wanting that base to be close to his only living relative. Sabrina loved having him near, though he was out of town as often as he was home.

Thinking of Colin made her wish her brother was home so she could call to ask him about Rob Davis. Who was the man and how did he know so much about her?

"Davis," she mused aloud, roaming around her apartment as she straightened a few things she'd left lying around in her rush to leave that morning.

"Davis." She thought back over twenty years of traveling in the wake of her wanderlust-infected father, a man who'd been incapable of remaining in one job for very long before boredom set in and he was off looking for another. Always certain the next opportunity would make him rich—somehow satisfy the ambiguous needs that drove him. Always moving from one state to another. Never more than a year in one place.

Her childhood memories slipped through her head like rushing water; different homes, different towns, strange children in unfamiliar classrooms, newly made friends waving goodbye, favorite toys lost in the shuffle, the worried look in her mother's eyes when her father had enthusiastically announced yet another job opportunity—another relocation. In his never-ending search for something he couldn't find, he was wholly unconscious of the sheer selfishness involved in uprooting his family again and again. He called it educational. His children, he would say, had seen it all.

And all Sabrina had ever wanted was a home, a friend she could keep for more than a scant few months, the same view out the same window every morning when she awoke.

She must have encountered dozens of people named Davis along the way. Dozens of Smiths and Joneses and Robinsons and Harrises. How was she supposed to remember them all? She couldn't even name all the towns they'd lived in before she'd finally escaped to college, only to fall in love with another nomad—a football player who spent the five years of their marriage being traded from one team to another. Unlike Sabrina's father, her husband couldn't even commit to one woman. He changed mistresses as easily as he changed teams. Too bad it had taken her five years to wise up.

Shaking her head with a scowl, she forced herself to stop thinking about Burt. How had her thoughts worked themselves around to her disastrous marriage?

The telephone rang just as she sat down on the living room couch. Reaching for it, she answered curiously. Who, other than Julia and Beverly, her two full-time office employees, knew she had come home early today? Had something already gone wrong at the office without her?

"Some people have no sense of responsibility at all. How dare you leave the office three whole hours early?"

The gently teasing voice made Sabrina smile. "Katherine! How did you know I was here?"

"I called your office. Julia's still in shock that you walked out."

"You'd think the *computer* had walked out."

"She probably thinks of you in much the same way as she does the computer," Katherine answered with a smile in her voice. "You're not going to deny that you have the slightest tendency toward workaholism, are you, Sabrina?"

"Workaholism?" Sabrina chuckled at the word, but didn't bother to deny it. They knew it applied—both to her and Katherine, actually.

"Actually, I'm just jealous that you have the option of taking off a few hours when you like. You know I've dreamed of being my own boss. So what are you going to do with the next few hours of freedom? Something wild and crazy?"

"I have no idea."

"Yeah, that's just about what I expected." Katherine sighed gustily. "I'm not sure you even remember how to be wild and crazy. The least you could do is go out and try to pick up a gorgeous man."

"Actually, a gorgeous man tried to pick *me* up in the elevator as I was leaving my office."

That got her friend's attention. "Details! Give me details."

Keeping her voice wryly amused, Sabrina told Katherine what had happened, leaving out nothing except her own confused reactions to Rob Davis's sexy smile and blue eyes.

"He knew all that about you and you can't remember him at all?" Katherine was definitely intrigued.

"He didn't even look vaguely familiar. I've never seen that man in my life."

"Why didn't you take him up on his offer of dinner? You could have tried to find out what was going on. Weren't you even curious?"

"Well, of course I was curious, but I couldn't just agree to have dinner with a stranger—a very odd stranger, at that."

"You could have met him in a crowded restaurant. You didn't have to give him your home address or anything."

"Still too dangerous. Besides, he . . . annoyed me," Sabrina added for lack of a better verb. She didn't know quite how to describe her feeling that Rob Davis could play havoc with her life if she gave him even the slightest hint of encouragement.

"Damn. Wish someone like that would come along to *annoy* me. I'd know what to do with him." Katherine sighed again when Sabrina refused to answer, then reluctantly changed the subject. "The reason I called was to ask if you want to have lunch with me Thursday. It's been weeks since we've had a chance to get together."

"I'd love to."

"Great. I'll give you a call Thursday morning to set time and place, okay?"

"Fine. I'll talk to you then."

"Have a nice afternoon, Sabrina. Even if you did blow your chance with the mystery hunk."

Sabrina replaced the receiver with a smile that quickly turned to a frown as she found herself wondering again about the man who'd introduced himself as Rob Davis. She'd drive herself crazy this way. And all she'd wanted to do was come home and enjoy a long, lazy afternoon doing absolutely nothing. Damn the man for interfering with her first afternoon off in months.

Feeling restless, she sat on the sofa, Angel curled at her feet, and tried to decide how to spend the remainder of the afternoon. She could go over the papers in her briefcase . . . No. She rejected that idea immediately. She was taking time off, she reminded herself. If she were going to work, she might as well have stayed at the office. She enjoyed her work, and was genuinely grateful that the opportunity to buy this business had presented itself at the same time her divorce settlement had been awarded, but there were times when even she needed a break. Today, for example.

Maybe she should have stopped by the mall, done some shopping. She supposed she could still throw on some jeans and a sweater and go. But the idea didn't really appeal to her. Shopping alone was something she did much too often.

Television? She picked up the remote control and turned on the set, settling more comfortably against the sofa cushions. Ten minutes later, she snapped the set off again, appalled at the selection of afternoon programming she'd discovered. Game shows designed to make fools of money-hungry contestants, soap operas with plot twists so intricate that one would have had to watch for years to understand who was doing what to whom, talk shows featuring bizarre guests, cartoons produced primarily to sell correlating merchandise. So much for daytime TV.

I think it's been much too long since you allowed yourself to play at all. What happened to you, Brie?

The memory of the quietly spoken observation made her groan. In response to the sound, Angel pushed an inquiring nose against her knee. Sabrina patted his sleek head. "It's okay, Angel. I was just assaulted by an irritating memory. Something ridiculous said by a pushy, ridiculous man."

In defiance of that persistent memory, she stood and walked determinedly up the stairs and into the spare bedroom, where a small desk in one corner held an expensive electronic typewriter and a stack of typed papers turned facedown in a neat pile. She had her hobby, just like everyone else, she thought rebelliously.

And then she had to be more honest with herself. Writing was hardly a hobby for her. More a passion, a need, an escape that had helped her go on during times when nothing else had seemed worthwhile for her. She'd been working on this particular story for nearly two years, in what little spare time she'd allowed herself away from the office. She supposed it could be classified as women's contemporary fiction—the tale of a woman who'd survived nearly impossible odds to found a business dynasty and who would find an equally strong, equally honorable man to love before the book ended.

No one other than her brother knew about Sabrina's writing, and even he had never read anything his sister had written. She didn't seriously imagine that she'd ever have the nerve to actually mail the manuscript to a publisher, risking yet another rejection, another broken dream. Writing was something she did for herself alone, a need she had that was fulfillment in itself. It was so much easier to indulge in safe, private daydreams of being published, having her work read and enjoyed, than it was to actually take the risk of going after that dream. So much less painful.

Reading over the last few pages she'd written a few weeks earlier, she frowned as she studied her description of the hero in her story. She'd made him blond and green-eyed. Chewing on her lower lip, she wondered if he'd be more interesting with jet black hair and bright blue eyes. Hmm.

Inserting a clean sheet of paper in the typewriter, she began to write, already lost in the joy of creating her own world, choosing just the right words to convey her thoughts. Seemingly satisfied with her familiar behavior, Angel rested his head on his front paws and closed his eyes.

2

ROB WAS WHISTLING when he entered his sister's house, still thinking about the unexpected reunion that afternoon. Sabrina Marsh. What were the odds of finding her again—in an elevator in a Dallas office building, of all places? He'd thought he was doing a good deed for his sister by delivering some papers to her accountant. He hadn't expected this little bonus for himself out of the gesture.

He found Liz sitting in the den, swollen feet propped on an ottoman as she studied a baby care book she held on the mound that had once been her lap. "Hey, Liz. Guess who I ran into in your accountant's office building. You'll never believe it."

Tilting her curly dark head, twenty-six-year-old Liz wrinkled her lightly freckled nose and tapped her chin with one finger, pretending to give serious consideration to his words. "I give up," she said at length, turning her blue eyes inquiringly toward him. "Who did you run into?"

"Sabrina Marsh." He produced the name with a verbal flourish, dropping into a nearby armchair to watch her reaction.

Liz frowned thoughtfully, her memory obviously tugged by the name, then widened her eyes. "Sabrina Marsh? I remember her!"

"Sure you do. You once thought she was pretty hot stuff. You used to imitate everything she did, wanting to be just like her when you became a teenager."

"I wasn't the one who had a major crush on her," Liz teased in return, grinning wickedly at her older brother. "It was you who used to leave candy bars anonymously on her doorstep. You were the one who once challenged her brother—who was quite a bit bigger than you at the time—to a fight for teasing her and making her cry."

Rob shrugged, clearing his throat somewhat uncomfortably. "Yeah, well, that's been a while."

"No kidding. What—seventeen years?"

He nodded. "At least."

"How'd you know it was her?"

He grinned. "She hasn't changed a bit. I mean, she's older of course and there are minor changes, but I still knew her the minute I saw her."

"I don't suppose she recognized you?"

He shook his head. "Not even a glimmer of recognition."

Liz ran her eyes affectionately down his mature, muscular frame. "Gee, what a surprise."

"I suppose I have changed more than she did. I didn't tell her how we knew each other before. I'm hoping curiosity will encourage her to have dinner with me one evening."

Liz closed her book and set it carefully aside. "You mean, like a date?"

"Yeah. Exactly like a date."

Looking skeptical, she eyed him. "She's older than you are, isn't she?"

He shrugged again. "Not enough to matter. She's still gorgeous. Classy, too. You'd have killed for the suit she had on."

Liz sighed gustily, patting her protruding stomach. "I'd kill for anything with a waistline right now," she admitted. "I'm really tired of wearing lace-trimmed parachutes."

"The joys of motherhood," he teased fondly, glancing at the place where his eagerly awaited niece or nephew rested.

"So you're really going to ask Sabrina Marsh out?" Liz asked, returning to the previous subject with all the determination of a naturally inquisitive younger sister.

"Already did. She shot me down. But you know me . . ."

Liz rolled her eyes and groaned. "Uh-huh. Never-say-die Rob. How do you know she's not married or engaged or something?"

"She'd have said if she were, wouldn't she?" he pointed out logically.

"So wear your uniform next time you ask her out. Something about Captain Robert S. Davis in dress blues turns normally intelligent women into drooling admirers. Can't imagine why, but it's been happening ever since you left the Air Force Academy."

Ignoring the faint heat in his cheeks, Rob scowled at Liz's taunting. "I don't think I'll have to resort to the uniform. Although I'll keep it in mind if all else fails."

"Got another plan, have you?"

He lifted his chin in deliberate cockiness. "Don't I always?"

"Oh, Lord. The woman had better run for the hills while she can."

Rob laughed. "I'm not that bad."

Liz only grimaced and shoved herself out of the deep chair, standing with the difficulty resulting from eight months of pregnancy. "I'm going to freshen up before Gordon comes home. Help yourself to a drink or whatever, okay?"

"Yeah, thanks."

He watched her waddle across the room, resisting the impulse to tease her about the uncharacteristic gracelessness of her movements. He knew she'd had just about enough of his pregnancy jokes.

Liz paused in the doorway and looked back over her shoulder. "So what is this determination of yours to go out with Sabrina? The fulfillment of a boyhood fantasy?"

"I guess you could call it that," he agreed equably.

"That's what I thought. Oh, well, if it gives you something to do besides count the minutes until you're back at that job you love so much, go for it. I've never seen you as restless as you've been during the past week, and you still have three weeks left of your leave time." With a smile, she left the room.

Rob winced. He hadn't realized his restlessness had shown so clearly to his family. Not that he wasn't enjoying his visit with them, of course, but he'd never been one to appreciate having empty time on his hands.

And then his thoughts turned back to Sabrina Marsh. As Liz had accused him, he'd had a major crush on Sabrina when she'd been fifteen. She hadn't looked twice at him, not that he'd have expected her to at the time. After all, he hadn't exactly moved in her social circles. But he'd definitely noticed her. She'd been the first person of the opposite sex to ever fully capture his adolescent attention.

Remembering the way his breath had caught when she'd looked at him in that elevator, he realized he'd never quite gotten over that crush, though he hadn't consciously thought of her in years. And, though time had put them on a more equal footing than they'd been before, she couldn't stand him now. He'd have to do something about that. Surely fate wouldn't give him another chance with her only to have it end like this.

His smile faded as he pictured her again. What had happened to her to take all the laughter out of her lovely silver-green eyes? And what would it take for him to put it back? Typically, he never questioned his ability to do so.

He rose from the chair and strolled across the room, digging into the small refrigerator behind the wet bar for the orange juice Liz kept there. He just happened to have three weeks to fill before leaving for Germany for a two-year tour of duty, three weeks that had stretched endlessly ahead of his impatient nature. It pleased him that he now had something to do during those weeks besides visit with his parents, run errands for his sister and count the days until he was back at work as an air force pilot.

He would use that free time to find out if the grown-up Sabrina Marsh was as fascinating as the teenager had been.

HER FINGERTIPS PRESSED against her temples, Sabrina pored over a stack of tax forms at her office the next morning, her brow creased as she tried to understand the complicated figures. Noises from the other offices penetrated the walls—telephones ringing, muffled voices, the copy machine being operated in the next room. She tried to block out those distractions, her full concentration on the figures in front of her. It all seemed so easy when her accountant went over it with her. So why did it seem so hard on her own?

"Excuse me, Sabrina, but there's someone here to see you."

Sabrina glanced up at her open office doorway, where Julia, her secretary-receptionist, stood smiling at her. She really didn't have time to see anyone, unless it was very important. These papers were due back at her accountant's office by one o'clock. She was going to have to skip lunch as it was. That's what she got, she thought resignedly, for taking a few hours off the day before. "Please tell whoever it is that I . . ."

". . . would be delighted to see him," a man's voice finished for her just as the owner of that voice stepped past Julia into Sabrina's office.

This time the attractive face with its engagingly cocky smile definitely looked familiar. She'd seen it only yesterday, when she'd left him standing in the parking lot looking after her as she'd driven away. "What are you doing here?"

Carrying a brightly colored gift bag, Rob Davis smiled over his shoulder at Julia as he approached Sabrina's desk. "Thanks, Julia. I'll take it from here."

Julia looked uncertainly at Sabrina. Whatever Rob had told her to make her usher him so confidently into her employer's office had obviously been brought into question by Sabrina's less than enthusiastic welcome. Though she fully intended to reprimand Julia later for being so gullible to a gorgeous male smile, she decided to be coolly professional in front of her uninvited caller. "Thank you, Julia. I'll let you know if I need anything."

Biting her lower lip, Julia turned and hurried away. Sabrina pushed her chair back and stood, hands spread on the glossy wood surface of her desk as she glared at Rob. It wasn't all that hard to understand why her impressionable young employee would have been willing to believe almost anything from this man. His short, dark hair sexily windblown, his tall, fit body clad in a clinging blue cotton sweater and pleated gray slacks, he could have stepped off the pages of a male fashion catalog. Hardly the type of man who usually entered the offices of Dial-a-Temp Inc.

"What," she repeated crisply, "are you doing here?"

"I came to see you," he replied, not noticeably daunted by her tone. "And to bring you a present." He set the bag in front of her.

She ignored it. "Mr. Davis, this is my place of business. I have work to do. I don't appreciate being interrupted."

"A temporary help service. Interesting. You own the business?"

"Yes, I do. And I'm quite busy, so . . ."

"You look lovely today. That suit is rather severe, but the green brings out the color of your eyes."

Becoming more and more angry with his persistence, she balled her fists when he made himself comfortable on one corner of her desk, looking at her with a blandly innocuous grin that made her long to hit him. Who did this guy think he was, anyway? "Must I call building security to have you removed from my office, Mr. Davis?"

He looked ridiculously wounded. "Brie. Would you really do that to an old friend?"

"We are not old friends!" she all but shouted in her frustration. And then she took a deep breath and lowered her voice. "I will repeat what I said yesterday. I don't know you. You do not look familiar to me. I don't recognize your name. Now why won't you leave me alone?"

"If you're so sure we've never met, how do you explain what's in that bag you're trying so hard to ignore?"

She looked suspiciously from him to the bag. "What is it?"

"I told you. A gift. Why don't you look inside?"

Hesitating a moment longer, she finally sighed in exasperation and snatched up the bag, opening it with carefully concealed curiosity. And then she frowned as she studied the contents. "How in the world—?"

The bag held a six-pack of canned root beer and a half dozen Three Musketeers bars.

The afternoon sun beat strongly on Sabrina's neck and back, bared by the skimpy bikini she wore as she sunbathed on a soft blanket, a melting candy bar and a warm can of root beer at her elbow. Lying on her stomach, crossed feet silently beating time to an Elton John rock song, she scribbled happily in her ever-present wirebound notebook. The tip of her ponytail tickled her nape and she tossed her head, then looked up from her notebook when she was distracted by the sound of her brother making bombing noises as he worked on a model military vehicle. The bushes rattled at the edge of the lawn and she scowled, wondering if the pesky neighborhood kids were spying on her again. But even that didn't spoil her pleasure in the afternoon. Gazing sightlessly into the distance, she allowed herself to daydream, imagining that she'd never have to leave here, that her father would finally be content to stay in one place, that the captain of the football team would finally notice her and ask her out. Dreaming . . .

"Well? Aren't you going to thank me for supplying you with your favorite snack food?"

Rob Davis's smug voice broke into the flash of memory, making Sabrina return to the present with a start. She deliberately converted her surprised expression to one of fierce determination. "Who *are* you?" she demanded, staring straight into his amused blue eyes.

"The man of your dreams," he quipped, reaching out to run one finger down the soft curve of her cheek.

Jerking away from his touch, Sabrina muttered her disgust with the arrogant reply. "You're not going to tell me the truth, are you?"

He managed to look wounded. "I thought I *was* telling the truth."

Realizing he still had no intention of explaining how they'd met, or how he just happened to know so much about her, she snatched up the bag and threw it at him. He caught it easily, demonstrating amazingly quick reflexes. "Out," she told him, pointing to the door.

Rob laughed. "Now, Brie—"

"I'm not joking. I want you out of my office. I have work to do."

"Don't you want to take the first of those three guesses I offered you? Surely my gift gave you some clue as to when we knew each other." His tone was tantalizing, challenging.

"I told you, I am not playing this game with you. Either you answer my questions or you can leave."

He shrugged negligently, placed the gift bag gently back on her desk and turned on one heel. "Okay. I'll be seeing you."

He was going? He really intended to leave her in mystified suspense? Dammit, she seethed, glaring at his retreating back, why was he doing this to her? "Irving," she heard herself saying impulsively, goaded into a desperate attempt to make sense of a situation that was rapidly turning her into a basket case.

Looking over his shoulder, Rob lifted an inquiring eyebrow. "I beg your pardon?"

She flushed, but continued doggedly. "Did we know each other when my family lived in Irving?"

His smile made her long to throw something else at him. Something large and heavy. "Could be," he murmured. "Is that your first guess?"

The impulse to clench her fists in her hair and scream was strong, but she resisted. Coating her voice with as much ice as she could manage, she replied. "No. I'm *not* playing your game. It was only a question."

"Okay. 'Bye, then." He closed her office door behind him when he left.

"Oooh," she whispered furiously, sinking into her chair and glowering at the offending gift bag as if it shared the guilt of its bearer. "That has to be the most obnoxious, aggravating, irritating—"

The door opened again. Rob poked his head around the edge. "Oh, by the way. Your first guess was correct. We did know each other in Irving."

He was gone before she could respond. Just as well, she decided. What she'd intended to say had certainly not been appropriate for the office. She contented herself with muttering juicy expletives between clenched teeth as she firmly settled back down to work, making a valiant effort to ignore the gaily decorated bag that seemed to laugh at her from the corner of her desk.

HE HAD DEFINITELY ticked her off. Ignoring the surreptitiously curious looks from the other three occupants of the elevator, Rob chuckled. He didn't know what, exactly, had happened to Sabrina Marsh during the past seventeen years or so, but he did know that it was long past time someone rattled her cage a bit. Cage. Now where had that word come from? Why did he have the odd hunch that Sabrina was a prisoner of her own daily routines?

Maybe she was perfectly happy with the way things were. Maybe she liked being all business, no nonsense, standoffish. If so, she'd changed a great deal more than he ever would have imagined. He could still remember her laughter, still remember the funny feeling in his stomach every time he'd heard it when he was a kid. Would he hear it again?

He grinned. Of course he would. He had no intention of conceding defeat at this point in the game.

THE BALLOONS ARRIVED late that afternoon, half a dozen huge bright yellow balloons tied with green ribbons.

Interrupted in the middle of discussing the following week's schedule with Beverly, Sabrina moaned when Julia carried the balloons in. Both her employees laughed at her expression.

"There's a card," Julia announced, pointing to the tiny envelope dangling from one of the ribbons.

"As if we don't know who sent them," Beverly teased. Having worked for Sabrina for nearly two years, she'd long since gotten over her original intimidation of her employer and had joined the ranks of friends who'd expressed concern about Sabrina's lack of an exciting social life. Still in her early twenties, and never lacking for interesting dates herself, the ebullient young woman had particularly scorned Sabrina's most recent escort—sober, sedate Daniel. "Surely there are most interesting single guys than that," she'd declared frankly after meeting Daniel.

Sabrina warily pulled the card from the envelope. "Yellow used to be your favorite color," the bold, decidedly masculine scrawl read. "These reminded me of the way the sunshine glittered in your hair yesterday. Have dinner with me tonight."

Realizing that her hand had lifted to her neatly upswept hair, Sabrina bit off a groan and immediately dropped her arm to her side. Damn the man. Didn't he know how to take no for an answer? And how was she supposed to decline his invitation, anyway? There was no phone number enclosed with the card.

"He's persistent, you can say that for him," Beverly commented carefully, her dark eyes alight with amusement as she studied the balloons floating above Sabrina's desk. Julia had told her all about Rob's unconventional visit earlier, including the fast-talking he'd done to get himself escorted into Sabrina's office without being announced.

"Good-looking, too, from the glimpse I caught of him this morning."

"He's becoming a serious problem," Sabrina replied quellingly.

Julia's round face creased in puzzled curiosity beneath her fringe of red bangs. "I know he was kind of pushy, but he's awfully good-looking. And he seemed nice. Great smile. Maybe you should go out with him. It might be fun."

Sabrina shook her head. "He's not my type."

Julia rolled her eyes expressively. "Come on, Sabrina. A guy like that is *every* woman's type."

"So go after him."

"You don't think I would if he'd shown any interest at all?" Julia retorted. "That man's only got eyes for you, boss."

"Then he'll just have to start looking in another direction. I'm tired of his silly guessing game, tired of these tantalizing little clues he keeps dropping, tired of . . ."

"What guessing game?" Beverly interrupted, visibly intrigued.

Catching herself, Sabrina shook her head again. "Never mind. Get Mallory Fraser on the phone for me, will you, Julia? I need to confirm with her that I have a clerical assistant lined up for her husband for next week. Then call Peggy and tell her that she'll need to report to Dr. Fraser's office by nine o'clock Monday morning. Oh, and, Beverly, I'd like to see the results of the office competency tests you gave this morning. I'm particularly interested in the first woman I interviewed, Hannah Steinberg."

Reluctant to drop the subject of Sabrina's unconventional suitor, Julia cast one last look at the cheerful balloon bouquet and then nodded. "Yes, ma'am." She turned and left, muttering to herself as she went. Beverly wasn't far behind, though her parting remarks were less subtle.

Sabrina was well aware that her employees were disgusted with her for being immune to Rob Davis's compelling charm. Or at least, Sabrina hoped she appeared to be immune. The truth was, she was having a harder time resisting than even she could believe. Some irritating little voice inside her kept urging her to give in, play along with Rob's game, go out with him, bask some more in the warmth of his dimpled smile. Thus far, she'd managed to ignore the voice, though she'd failed to eliminate it.

She had very good reasons to continue to resist Rob Davis. She didn't know him, despite his taunting claims to the contrary. She didn't trust him. And she didn't trust her own reactions to him. Something about him made her wary, nervous, unwillingly agitated. He was the type of man to stir fantasies in any woman, and she'd learned firsthand how painful such fantasies could be in the end. She'd made a decision long ago, after her divorce, to avoid such pain in the future. She wasn't going to change her mind now.

HE WAS STANDING beside the elevator when she left her office for the day. Leaning against the wall, arms crossed comfortably over his broad chest, he looked as if he were prepared to wait quite a while. He looked so handsome her knees weakened, though she made sure nothing more than mild annoyance showed on her face. She already felt foolish with the huge cluster of balloons bobbing above and behind her. She hadn't quite known what to do with them, hadn't wanted to leave them in her office. They seemed so terribly out of place there. So unprofessional.

"Go away," she said before he could speak, viciously punching the call button.

Rob only chuckled. "I'll have to take the elevator to do that. Mind if I share yours?"

"Yes. I do mind."

The doors slid open, revealing two unsmiling men in conservative suits staring impassively forward. Her cheeks flaming, Sabrina stepped into the car, navigating the balloons beneath the doorway. Rob was right behind her, as she'd known he would be.

Grinning broadly, he batted a balloon away from his face as the car began to descend. One of the other men sighed impatiently and backed into a corner when a trailing green ribbon tickled his neck. Sabrina's face burned even hotter. "Here," she said impulsively, thrusting her handful of balloon strings at Rob. "You do something with them. You're the one responsible for them."

He looked meditatively at the balloons that filled most of the upper half of the elevator, then shrugged and reached into his pocket. Pulling out a small pocket knife, he flipped it open with one hand. "Okay. I'll get rid of them if you want me to."

"No!" Without even knowing why she did it, she snatched the strings away from him, clutching them as if to protect them from danger. For some reason, she just couldn't stand to watch him stab the gaily bobbing yellow balloons. She knew it was foolish, but it almost seemed like murder.

His smile broadening, Rob closed his knife and slid it back into his pocket. "What time should I pick you up for dinner?"

"When hell freezes over," she snapped in return, then wished she'd come up with something more original.

"Now, Brie . . ."

Miserably aware of the interest they were receiving from their two elevator companions, she almost sighed in relief when the doors opened to the lobby. She hurried out, apologizing in a mutter to a woman whose hat was nearly knocked off by a straying balloon.

"Brie," Rob said again, easily keeping up with her as she hurried toward the revolving doors. "What is it about me that you find so annoying?"

She threw him a narrowed look. "I would think you'd be used to that reaction by now, given your personality."

He winced, but didn't pause. "Some people think I've got a great personality," he informed her. "I'm charming, witty, very intelligent, I'm kind to animals, children and old people and I call my mother once a week. What's not to—?"

His words were cut off when she stepped into the revolving door, fighting to squeeze the balloons into the wedge-shaped space with her. Thinking it was a miracle she'd made it through without popping any of them, she hurried out onto the sidewalk.

"You want to know what I think?" The words came from just behind her right shoulder.

"Not particularly." She kept walking, spotting her car with great relief.

He ignored her response, as she should have expected. "I think you're intrigued by me. I think you might even be just the tiniest bit attracted to me. And that makes you very nervous, because I'm a puzzle to you. I don't quite fit the safe, dull routine you've fallen into. You've created this image of a no-nonsense professional businesswoman and you're afraid to admit that there's still a part of you that likes games and puzzles and taking risks."

Appalled by his accusations, Sabrina whirled to face him, back pressed against her car, balloon strings clutched in one fist, purse and briefcase held to her chest like a shield with the other hand. "You're crazy, do you know that? I am *not* intrigued by you. I am *not* attracted to you. And for the last time, I am *not* playing your stupid—"

The last word died in a strangled choke when his mouth covered hers. Pressed against the car as she was, both hands full, there was little she could do except stand rigidly as he kissed her.

Okay, so she'd been lying about not being intrigued by him. And she'd been lying about not being attracted to him. And he'd been absolutely correct about her being afraid to do anything about it. The urge to let go of the balloon strings, drop her purse and briefcase, throw both arms around his neck and kiss him back terrified her. How did he *do* this to her?

The kiss was only a brief one, though for all Sabrina knew it could have lasted hours. He just touched her lips with his mouth. Yet she was trembling when he stepped back, her heart racing in her chest. She tried to tell herself the reaction was caused solely from temper. She knew she was lying again. "Why did you do that?"

"Sorry," he murmured, not looking at all repentant. "I couldn't resist. You wouldn't believe how long I've wanted to kiss you."

She only stared at him.

One corner of his mouth quirked upward in a ridiculously wistful smile. "Are you sure you aren't just the tiniest bit attracted to me?"

She straightened to her full height and lifted her chin, refusing to dignify that with a reply.

"I'm more than a little attracted to you," he went on conversationally. "Believe me, this isn't something I do all the time. I know you think I'm crazy—hell, maybe I am—but I haven't been able to stop thinking about you since I saw you again yesterday."

His words stunned her, though she tried to believe they were only a well-worn line. "Why won't you tell me how we met?" she asked huskily.

Rob suddenly looked sheepish. "Maybe I'm not too eager to have you remember."

"I knew it!" she exclaimed. "You *are* someone I didn't like!"

"Oh, you liked me, I think," he answered reflectively. And then his quick grin returned. "After all, what's not—"

"—to like," she finished with him, sighing. The man had an ego that just didn't quit. So why was she suddenly finding it harder to resist him?

He's not my type, she reminded herself sternly, picturing the last man she'd had dinner with, a couple of weeks earlier. Daniel McDougal, fifty, conservative, widowed, brilliant. And well, just a little dull. But at least with him she didn't feel so...so out of control. So uncertain. So damned *girlish*. She was thirty-three years old, for pity's sake. What was it about Rob Davis that made her feel like a blushing teenager again?

She really hated that feeling. Didn't she? Of course she did, she thought decisively. "Goodbye, Mr. Davis."

"Have dinner with me, Brie."

"No."

"I'm prepared to beg."

She wouldn't smile, she thought quickly, forcing her lips to cooperate. She wouldn't give in to that silly, lopsided grin of his. "It wouldn't do you any good."

"I'm not going to give up, you know."

"Neither am I." She turned firmly to her car, then swallowed a curse when she found herself juggling keys, briefcase, purse and balloon strings.

"Here." His voice was warm with amusement. "Let me help." Reaching around her, he took the keys and opened her door, helping her guide the balloons into the small car.

"Thank you," she said without looking at him.

"You're welcome." He stepped back. "See you around, Brie."

"Not if I can help it," she muttered, crawling behind the wheel and slamming the car door between them. Pushing the balloons out of the way as best she could, she backed out of the parking space and left him standing in the same spot where she'd left him the day before. Only this time she was fully aware that she'd be seeing him again. And to her utter dismay she realized that some foolish part of her was rather looking forward to it.

3

"HI, SABRINA." The squeaky young voice greeted her the moment she stepped out of her car in her driveway. "Wow, neat balloons."

Sabrina looked over to the neighboring apartment of the duplex where a pretty ten-year-old with long tawny braids was sitting in a wheelchair on the tiny front porch. "Hi, Mandy. What are you doing?" she greeted her young neighbor fondly, walking up the porch and leaning against a post.

"I'm waiting for Daddy. He had a meeting this afternoon but he's 'sposed to be home soon. I have something real important to tell him."

"You do?" Sabrina asked encouragingly, smiling at the child. Born with cerebral palsy, Mandy was a bright, happy little girl whom anyone would love. After watching her grow for three years, Sabrina adored her. The feeling was quite mutual, though Sabrina sometimes suspected she came second to her dog in Mandy's affections.

"Uh-huh. I got an A on my math test today. One hundred per cent!" Mandy announced proudly, her excitement causing her head to bob dramatically. Mandy had limited control of her muscles, which meant she would never walk and she sometimes made unrestrained movements, but her intelligence was well above normal for her age. Her parents made sure her life was as close to an average childhood as possible.

"Oh, Mandy, I'm so proud of you! Here," she said impulsively, tying the strips of the balloons to one arm of the wheelchair, "these are for you."

Her head bobbing even more in her excitement, Mandy grinned from ear to ear, her voice rising nearly an octave. "Thank you! Oh, they're so pretty. They look like sunshine."

These reminded me of the way the sunshine glittered in your hair. Sabrina found herself blushing for absolutely no reason that she could imagine as the words from the card popped into her mind.

The card. "Oops. Wait just a second," she told Mandy, digging among the green ribbons to detach the card that still dangled from one of them. "I'll keep this."

Mandy giggled. "I bet it's a love note, isn't it, Sabrina? You've got a boyfriend, haven't you?"

"Mandy," chided a woman's voice from the doorway behind them. "Please try not to embarrass our landlady."

"Hi, Ellen." Sabrina looked up with a weak smile as Mandy's mother opened the storm door and stepped out to join them.

A plain, likable woman a year older than Sabrina, Ellen O'Neal had mousy brown hair tied back from her face and the thick glasses she wore had a smudge of flour on one lens, that almost concealed the lively brown eye behind it. She pulled the glasses off and absently wiped them on her apron. "Hello, Sabrina."

"How are things at the university?" Sabrina asked to make conversation. Ellen was a professor of mathematics, her husband a professor of history, both employed at SMU.

"As hectic as always at this time of the year," Ellen replied, replacing her glasses. "Spring fever is near epidemic proportions."

Sabrina just managed not to wince. Maybe that was *her* problem, she thought ruefully. Maybe she was suffering from a touch of spring fever herself for the first time in years.

"I see your father's car, Mandy," Sabrina said, stepping toward her own porch. "Now you can tell him about your math test. I have to go in before Angel tears down my door. He's been whining in there for the past ten minutes."

Her gaze turning reluctantly from her balloons, Mandy smiled in response. "I hear him. Can he come visit later?"

"Of course he can."

"See you, Sabrina."

"See you, sweetie." Smiling, Sabrina let herself into her apartment, the card from Rob still clutched in one hand.

IT HAD BEEN a very long time since Sabrina had had an erotic dream. She had one that night. Rob was kissing her again, his mouth moist, sun-warmed, hungry, just as it had been in the parking lot. Only this time he also touched her with his hands, running them over her throbbing, eager, nude body with a skill that made her writhe and moan in pleasure. And she touched him in return, thrusting her fingers into his short, crisp dark hair, tracing his long, masculine dimples with the tip of her tongue, nibbling at the slight cleft in his chin, testing the strength of his broad shoulders and muscular arms.

She awoke with a gasp and a shudder, her body aching, actually craving a man's touch for the first time in longer than she could remember. She'd put all her energy since the end of her marriage into her education and then her career, leaving little time or inclination for socializing. Perhaps her body was reminding her that she had other needs besides a successful career.

So why couldn't her suddenly demanding hormones have kicked in when she'd been out with Daniel, who'd have been more than happy to satisfy her desires? Why not with any of the other safe, reliable, conservative men she'd dated in the past few years? Why did it have to be Rob Davis who'd appeared in her dream, who turned her knees to jelly, whose lazy smiles lured her into that dangerously unreliable world of fantasy?

"Way to go, Sabrina," she muttered aloud, her voice thoroughly disgruntled in the darkness. "Eligible men everywhere and you have to fixate on an obnoxious man with questionable sanity. How discriminating of you."

Determined to go back to sleep—dreamlessly—she closed her eyes. Only to be assaulted again by a vision of Rob Davis, standing in the sunshine, smiling down at her.

She groaned and pulled her pillow over her head as if that would block out the annoyingly enticing memory.

SABRINA WAS STILL TRYING to forget her uncomfortable dream when she walked into a pizza parlor close to her office the next day. At one o'clock, most of the luncheon crowd had thinned, which was why she and her friend Katherine Fuller had chosen to meet at that time. Sabrina spotted Katherine immediately, as the tall, striking brunette was waving from a cozy booth in one corner of the colorfully decorated room.

"Have you ordered yet?" Sabrina asked, sliding into the opposite side of the booth.

Katherine shook her dark head, causing her stylishly blunt cut hair to sway at her jawline. "I just got here, myself. Should we be sensible and have the salad bar or fall off the wagon and split a pizza?"

Sabrina always had the salad bar. Sabrina was always sensible. "Let's order a pizza," she heard herself saying.

Looking rather surprised, as if she really hadn't expected Sabrina's response, Katherine motioned for a waitress. The personnel director of a large insurance company, she had met Sabrina through business, but both had quickly become more than professional acquaintances. They had a great deal in common; both were in their early thirties, comfortably established in their fields, unmarried and in no hurry to change that status. They'd become close friends during the past couple of years, getting together frequently to compare notes on the lives of single businesswomen.

"Hungry today?"

Sighing, Sabrina rested her elbow on the tabletop and propped her chin in her hand. "Maybe I'm just tired of always being sensible."

"Well, hallelujah, Hannah, strike up the band."

Amused by her friend's cheery comment, Sabrina laughed softly. "What was that supposed to mean?"

"That means," Katherine explained gravely, "that it's about time you did something frivolous for a change. Even if it's only ordering a pizza instead of a salad or taking an afternoon off from work, the way you did Tuesday."

Sabrina snorted delicately. "You're one to talk."

Katherine nodded in acknowledgement of the point. "I know. We're very much alike in some ways. But you have to admit that I do cut loose more often than you do, even if it is only once a year or so."

Chuckling, Sabrina sipped her ice water, then ran a fingertip down the condensation-beaded side of the plastic tumbler as she studied the woman across the table. "Okay, so you indulge in an occasional weekend of debauchery. Why, just last summer you took a Caribbean cruise—only to participate in a bridge tournament being held on board ship all weekend."

Katherine made a face at Sabrina's mocking accusation. "So it wasn't a trip down the fast lane. But at least," she added meaningfully, "I wasn't alone on the cruise. You do remember my bridge partner, don't you?"

Sabrina rolled her eyes. "Of course I do. Benjamin Lassiter Montgomery the Fourth. Wealthy, distinguished, divorced three times and old enough to be your father. He had to interrupt the bridge tournament every half hour to take a heart pill, didn't he?"

Cheeks darkening, Katherine squirmed in her vinyl seat. "Every hour and a half."

Her point well made, Sabrina allowed the subject to lapse. She shook out her napkin and placed it across her lap as their waitress slid a thickly topped pizza on the table between them. "Time for serious sinning."

"For you, maybe," Katherine muttered. "I could think of better things to do if I happened to be in the mood to be bad."

"A rousing game of horseshoes, perhaps?" Sabrina inquired sweetly.

"Okay, okay, forget I brought it up." Katherine held both hands palm outward in laughing surrender. "I'm no wilder than you are. Let's face it, we're duds."

"I think I resent that," Sabrina grumbled, but something about the rich aroma of the pizza robbed the complaint of its sting. She took a large bite, steaming cheese stringing from the thick crust, her eyes closing in near ecstasy. "Oh, my," she said when she'd swallowed the first heavenly bite. "That's better than sex."

Katherine lifted one skeptical eyebrow.

Sabrina only laughed softly. "As far as I can remember," she added and sank her teeth into the pizza again.

Someone dropped change into the juke box in the corner behind Sabrina's seat, followed by the opening chords of one of her all-time favorite "oldies" songs. She smiled. Pizza and Elton John. Maybe it wasn't the fast lane, but she had no complaints at the moment. Nothing could destroy the simple pleasure of this luncheon with her friend.

"You know," Katherine murmured dreamily, her dark eyes focused somewhere over Sabrina's left shoulder. "Even I might be tempted to try something wild with a man like that. Talk about sin-on-the-hoof!"

Without much interest, Sabrina mumbled an incoherent response around a swallow of pepperoni and mushrooms.

Katherine's eyes widened. "He's looking this way. Staring right at us."

"Big deal. We're the only women in the place who don't have children with us."

"I guess you're right. But he's smiling—oh, honey, what a smile!—as if he knows something we don't know. I wonder what he's thinking."

Her curiosity finally aroused, Sabrina looked casually over her shoulder. And promptly choked on her pizza. Grabbing frantically for her water glass, she gulped half the contents in an effort to clear her suddenly tight throat.

What was Rob Davis doing in this pizza parlor, leaning negligently against the juke box, looking as if he were prepared to spend the rest of the day just standing there watching her?

"Sabrina?" Katherine leaned forward in concern at her friend's odd behavior. "Are you all right?"

Lifting her hand to her flushed cheek, Sabrina slowly shook her head. "No. I'm not all right. *Damn* that man. Not only does he invade my bedroom, he even has to ruin the first truly enjoyable lunch I've had in ages."

Dark eyes going wide with avid interest, Katherine clasped her hands in front of her, their half-eaten pizza forgotten. "He invaded your bedroom? Now this I have to hear!"

Realizing what she'd said, Sabrina could have bitten her tongue. "It's not what that sounded like," she muttered, deeply embarrassed. How could she possibly explain?

Katherine looked disappointed. "Oh. You mean you don't know him?" And then her eyes brightened as she did some mental calculations. "You mean *he's* the guy you told me about—?"

"No," Sabrina cut in flatly, sensing Rob's approach and making quite sure her voice carried to him. "I *don't* know him. Despite what he says to the contrary."

"Really, Brie, you're going to bruise my ego if you don't stop rebuffing me this way," Rob commented, sliding into the booth beside her as if he'd been expected all along.

"Impossible." Her tone made her skepticism clear. "An ego the size of yours can't be bruised. I couldn't dent it with a sledgehammer. You followed me here from my office, didn't you?"

"That's what I love most about her," Rob said to Katherine, ignoring Sabrina's question, his voice deep with suppressed amusement. "She's such a sweet talker."

He stretched an arm across the back of the red vinyl booth, just brushing Sabrina's shoulders. She leaned slightly forward, breaking the contact. Even that brief touch had caused her nerve endings to quiver. Dream memories haunted her, taunted her. Was his skin really as warm and sleek as she'd imagined it? His arms like hot steel? His kisses as—

Stop this! she silently screamed to all her raging instincts, even as Rob casually introduced himself to Katherine. "Sabrina and I have known each other for years," he added with a wicked grin that dared Sabrina to contradict him.

Katherine looked enchanted. "But Sabrina said—"

"As far as I'm concerned, I met this man the day before yesterday when he accosted me in an elevator," Sabrina broke in again. "He claims we knew each other before, but he's demented, poor thing. The only reason I haven't called the police to make him stop harassing me is that I've always been sympathetic to the mentally ill. My sympathy, however, is about to run out."

"She's terrific, isn't she?" Rob asked Katherine, his sexy grin broadening as he helped himself to a slice of pizza. "Have you known her long?"

"A couple of years," Katherine answered, smiling as she looked from Sabrina to Rob with avid interest.

Rob swallowed a third of his purloined pizza slice in one bite, then asked, "Ever known her to be completely rattled?"

"No, I can't say that I have."

"Wouldn't you say it's about time?"

"Yes," Katherine answered, suddenly thoughtful. "I think it is."

"Katherine!"

Katherine only smiled at Sabrina's exclamation. "Sorry, Sabrina. But you know that's exactly what I was trying to tell you before Rob joined us."

"Was it?" Rob looked delighted. He turned to Sabrina. "See? Even your friend thinks I'd be good for you. So now will you go out with me?"

"Are your feet cold?" she asked in return.

He looked a little disconcerted, which pleased her very much since it was usually the other way around. "Well—no," he admitted.

She smiled limpidly. "Then I don't suppose hell has frozen over yet, do you?"

Rob gave an approving laugh and dropped his outstretched arm around her shoulders to hug her to his side.

"Damn, but I like you. Come on, Brie, say you'll have dinner with me. What could it hurt?"

"The man's only asking you to dinner, Sabrina," Katherine pointed out. "Give it a chance."

"I really don't think he needs any help, Katherine."

"Don't believe it, Katherine. I need all the help I can get." Rob's arm tightened briefly around Sabrina's shoulders, then he released her. "Well?"

She looked at him for a long moment, frowning. "Are you going to stop asking if I say no this time?"

"Not a chance."

"That's what I thought." She sighed. Somewhere, she thought with grim humor, the devil was reaching for his overcoat. "All right, Rob, I'll have dinner with you. On one condition."

"I won't try anything funny," he promised, one hand lifted in the Boy Scout sign of honor.

"You can bet your dimples you won't try anything funny," she returned coolly. "But that wasn't the condition."

"What is it?"

"Tell me how we met."

He winced, then hesitated. "I'll tell you—when the time is right."

She didn't like that at all, but it was time to go back to her office and she really needed to get away from him to think about what she'd just let herself in for by agreeing to go out with him. She couldn't think clearly with him sitting so close to her. She could hardly remember her name with him sitting so close to her. "Pick me up tonight at eight." Might as well get this over with, she thought in resignation.

"Seven," he amended quickly, then smiled with mock innocence. "I'd be starving by eight."

"All right, seven," she agreed, surrendering once again. "I live at—"

"I know where you live," he assured her. Then, at her look of surprise, explained, "I looked it up in the phone book."

Of course he had. Sabrina grabbed her purse and waited pointedly for him to stand so she could slide out of the booth. He finished the last bite of his pizza, washed it down with a healthy sip from her water glass, then shoved himself to his feet. "Nice to meet you, Katherine. Thanks for the help."

"You're welcome. And, by the way, if this doesn't work out, Sabrina has my number."

Rob grinned. "I'll remember that." He waited until Sabrina had told her friend goodbye, then took her arm. "I'll walk you back to your office."

"That's really not necessary."

"It's no trouble at all," he assured her gravely. "Besides, I'm parked there."

She gave up, knowing she might as well. She did start to protest, however, when Rob threw some money on the table. "Lunch was on me," he announced, overriding her objection, "since I so rudely interrupted your visit."

"No argument from me," Katherine agreed cheerfully, purse tucked under her arm as she walked with them as far as the door. "Though it would have been worth the money just to watch the two of you together."

Sabrina glared at the other woman and kept her mouth shut.

Rob seemed content to walk quietly at her side as they returned to her office building. He left her on the sidewalk at the revolving door. "I'm looking forward to tonight," he told her, catching her arm to detain her for a moment.

She wasn't sure what to say in reply. She couldn't exactly say she was looking forward to the date. She only wished she could call up just a bit more reluctance.

He leaned over to brush her mouth very lightly with his. "See you tonight, Brie."

And then he turned and left her staring after him, a reversal from their usual pattern.

He really had to stop doing that, she told herself, pushing through the revolving door into her office building. Those kisses of his could easily become addictive.

A DINNER DATE. *It's only a dinner date.* Sabrina stood staring into her closet, the rows of multicolored garments swirling before her in a rainbow haze. No big deal. She often went out for dinner with men. And this particular date would end just as all those others ended—on her front doorstep.

So what was wrong with her? she asked herself with a groan, clenching her fists in her disheveled hair. She never spent half an hour staring into her closet, trying to decide what to wear for an ordinary dinner date.

She'd known all along to avoid this. She'd tried, she really had tried. Rob Davis didn't belong in her safe, ordinary, routine life. He was a total stranger, and he was already wreaking havoc with her concentration. Hardly conscious of her choice, she jerked an emerald-green silk dress from its padded hanger and threw it recklessly onto the bed, digging into her wardrobe for lingerie and accessories.

She was ready at five minutes before seven. Inspecting her reflection in a full-length mirror, she told herself she looked just right for this particular date. The silk dress was flattering, figure-forming, yet cut severely enough to give her a slightly intimidating air when combined with her neatly upswept hair and expensive, unobtrusive gold jewelry. She was satisfied that there was nothing about her appearance to hint at the nerves that quivered beneath the composed facade.

And then the doorbell rang and she almost jumped out of her neat black pumps. Hand on her fluttering heart, she counted to thirty before turning on one heel and leaving her bedroom, descending the stairs to the living room where Angel barked furiously at the door.

"Get back, Angel," she ordered automatically, relieved to hear that her voice, at least, sounded normal. Glancing by habit through the small, diamond-shaped window in the door, she flipped the locks as her eyes met Rob's through the glass. "Come in, Rob."

"Sure I won't be eaten alive if I do?" he asked cautiously, looking around her to the large, bristling black dog sitting behind her.

"You won't be eaten unless I give the command," she replied, unable to resist smiling.

"That's supposed to be reassuring?"

"Let's just say I have no plans to sic him on you—at the moment, anyway." She stepped back to allow him to enter. As he passed her, Sabrina automatically noted the way his dark blue suit clung to his muscular shape, her eyes lingering on the width of his shoulders. She deliberately shut down the fantasy memories those wonderful shoulders evoked.

She smiled brightly, falsely, determined to ease the awkwardness she felt over this supposedly ordinary dinner date. "Are you ready to tell me who you are?"

"Not just yet," Rob answered with a grin at her curiosity. "Are you ready to go?"

Sabrina frowned. "I must have deliberately blocked you out of my mind because you're so annoying!"

"Maybe you did," he agreed equably. "You once told me I could be a pest at times."

"I did? When?" she demanded, her fists on her hips.

He shrugged, refusing to answer.

"I don't believe you."

Rob stepped closer, lifting her chin on the edge of his hand. "I never lie, Sabrina."

She was the first to look away. "I suppose I have to believe you, then," she said, stepping back from his disturbing proximity. She just couldn't deal with the strange effects of Rob's touch at the moment.

Her backward movement bumped her into Angel, and she looked down in surprise, realizing that the dog hadn't protested when Rob had touched her. Angel didn't usually allow strangers to touch his mistress without a softly growled warning. Did Angel somehow sense that Sabrina knew she was in no physical danger from Rob?

Rob's gaze followed Sabrina's. "What a beauty," he approved warmly. "Why don't you introduce us?"

She patted her pet's lean back. "This is Angel. My roommate."

Only after Sabrina had spoken the dog's name did Rob extend his hand, and then he didn't touch Angel, but waited patiently to be sniffed and evaluated. Angel made a rapid inspection of the friendly stranger, panting up into Rob's face with obvious invitation, to which Rob responded by patting the noble head and scratching obligingly behind the pointed ears. "Hello, Angel."

"He likes you," Sabrina remarked unnecessarily, since Angel was aptly expressing his own opinion with enthusiastic wiggles. *Traitor*, she thought, deciding to have a long talk with the dog later about who should and should not be trusted. Who'd have thought her dog would fall for a sexy smile?

Rob looked up with a one-sided grin that made him look suddenly very young and devastatingly handsome. "What's not to like?" he quipped, the repetition rapidly becoming a private joke between them, increasing the strange sense of intimacy that surrounded them in her living room.

Aware of a compelling urge to clear her throat, Sabrina returned the smile somewhat shakily and turned to find her purse. Oh, the man was dangerous! If she weren't careful, she'd end up making a bigger spectacle of herself than her usually dignified pet, who was even now squirming closer to Rob for more attention. An unnerving picture flashed into her mind of those strong, tanned hands caressing her body as they were even now stroking Angel. Dear heaven, what had gotten into her?

Rob's car turned out to be a low-slung, racy black model. If she'd had to guess what he drove, she would have imagined a car exactly like this one, she mused, climbing carefully into it. So very different from the more sedate businessmen's vehicles her older, less dashing dates drove.

"Do you like Italian food well enough to have it again tonight, even though you had pizza for lunch?" Rob asked, starting the powerful engine. "I'm in the mood for one of those places where they bring you a different course every few minutes until I think I'm going to die from overeating."

Sabrina smiled. "Sounds wonderful."

"A woman after my own heart," he quipped, guiding the car down the street. "Wanna get married?"

She laughed at the cheerfully teasing question, then sobered abruptly as something occurred to her. "I never even thought to ask if you were married!" She usually made a point of inquiring about a man's marital status *before* accepting a date with him.

"Now how could I propose to you if I were already married?" Rob asked with amused logic. "I assure you I'm single. Always have been."

"You never even asked if I were married," she commented, remembering his single-minded determination to ask her out from practically the moment he'd seen her in the elevator.

"You would have told me if you were. Have you ever been?"

"I was married for five years. A long time ago. I've been divorced for nearly seven years now."

"No children, I assume?"

"No children." Burt hadn't wanted any; the fact that Sabrina did hadn't particularly mattered to him. She pushed down a wave of old resentment, and quickly changed the subject. "Did we go to school together in Irving?"

Rob smiled, guiding the car into a parking space outside the popular Italian restaurant he'd chosen. "Is that your second guess?"

"It's just a question, dammit."

He chuckled at her obvious frustration. "I'll answer it, anyway. We were both students when we knew each other before."

"That's not much of an answer."

He grinned. "No, but I've got your full attention, don't I?" he inquired whimsically. And then he reached for his door handle. "Let's eat."

4

ROB GAVE SABRINA little chance to ask questions over dinner. She was too busy answering his. He seemed intent on finding out all there was to know about her, apparently fascinated by everything she said. At his questioning, she admitted that she'd been working her way through college when she'd met her ex-husband, a minor-talent professional football player. Burt had been handsome, charming, fun, and Sabrina had been swept off her feet. After five years of following him as he was traded from one team to another, sitting on the sidelines watching him play, and enduring the knowledge that his marriage vows had hardly held until the honeymoon was over, she'd found the nerve to leave him and strike out on her own.

"You must have worked very hard to get where you are now," he murmured, his hand hovering over an antipasto tray containing assorted fruits and cheeses, prosciutto and lemon-marinated shrimp.

"Very," she answered, not glossing over the facts.

"Why a temporary help service? How did you get into that?"

"I worked for a similar business while I attended college, before Burt and I married. I enjoyed it, found it very interesting to work with so many different types of people. I saw a real demand for the business, both for companies who need temporary help and for people who need part-time jobs or who are looking for a means to support themselves until a full-time job comes along. When Burt and I settled our property after the divorce, I had some money to invest in my future. Dial-a-Temp was the investment I chose."

"How many employees do you have?"

"Two full-time in my office and we have thirty-five temps registered at the moment, though that number varies. I'm considering adding another full-time associate in the office to assist with testing, interviewing and scheduling. Right now we specialize in clerical office help, but I'm thinking about expanding into other areas—warehouse and assembly line, janitorial, that sort of thing."

"Any regrets about buying the business?"

She shook her head. "None."

He studied her face for a long moment while a smiling waiter set their first course in front of them, tender conchiglioni filled with a spicy spinach and ricotta mixture. Sabrina wondered what Rob was thinking so seriously, but before she could ask, he changed the subject, asking about Colin. Sabrina told him a little about Colin's job as a freelance photographer. "We're very close," she added. "We don't get to see each other enough because his job takes him away so often."

When did you lose your mother?" he asked, his voice gentle.

It still hurt, she found. "Eight years ago."

"You were married then."

"Yes."

"I'm glad you weren't alone."

She only shrugged. She hadn't been alone, but only because Colin had been there for her to cry with. Burt had been too busy with his own pursuits to do more than offer surface sympathy to his grieving wife. That had been about the time Sabrina had realized the marriage was doomed to failure, though she'd tried for several more months to make it work, reluctant even then to admit defeat.

Rob waited a few moments for her to speak, then when she remained silent, asked, "What about your father?"

"He died when I was a senior in high school," she answered, knowing her voice held little emotion.

"I'm sorry." And then, as if sensing her need to change the subject again, he did. "What do you do when you're not working?"

"I take some graduate courses," she admitted. "And I like spending an occasional evening out with friends. But I also enjoy staying at home, spending time with good books and Angel. Did I tell you that I own my home? I rent the other half to a very nice couple with an adorable daughter."

"You're doing quite well for yourself," he commented as he reached for the valpolicella wine he'd ordered to accompany their meal. He sipped it slowly, waiting for her response.

Sabrina shrugged, knowing he was right. Feeling like a fool after the disaster of her marriage, she'd put away childish dreams and fantasies and dedicated herself to becoming a responsible, self-reliant adult. She counted herself fortunate that she'd learned life's hard lessons so early. She was in control of her life now, and that included her relationships with men.

Yes, she *was* doing well for herself, by herself. "We've been talking about me all evening. What do you do, Rob?"

"I'm a pilot."

Intrigued, she cocked her head and looked across the table, picturing him at the yoke of an airplane. Studying those attractive fine lines at the corners of his eyes, she realized that they'd been caused more by hours of squinting into the sun than by the passage of years. "How interesting. I don't know any other professional pilots. Do you fly for one of the major airlines?"

"The biggest," he replied with a smile. "Uncle Sam's."

Unaccountably startled, she abruptly put down the wineglass she'd just lifted halfway to her mouth. "You're in the service?"

His grin widened as he sketched a flourishing bow without rising from his chair. "Captain Robert S. Davis, United States Air Force, at your service, ma'am."

"Oh." She stared at her plate.

"What's wrong?"

Blinking, she shook her head and forced a smile. "Why, nothing. I was just surprised, that's all."

Another nomad, she thought with a deep sense of regret. Why did she always seem to be attracted to them? If she'd had any budding fantasies about something coming of her attraction to Rob, he'd just settled that. The U.S. Air Force wasn't exactly known for allowing its members to establish themselves in one place and stay there. "Are you stationed in Texas?" she asked, already sensing his answer somehow.

He shook his head. "No. I'm on a month's leave prior to being reassigned. I'm taking the time to visit with my family."

Just passing through. "Oh." She looked away. "Oh, good. Here's our second course."

As if in repayment of his interrogation of her, Rob cooperatively submitted to Sabrina's questions about his career. "How long have you been flying?" she asked, pushing away her disappointment with his revelation and determining to enjoy the remainder of her evening, since it would probably be the last she'd spend with him.

"Since I was sixteen. It was something I wanted to do for as long as I can remember. My parents could hardly hold me back until I was old enough. Other guys asked for a car for their sixteenth birthdays—I got flying lessons. Didn't get a car of my own until I graduated high school."

She smiled. "Didn't that interfere with your social life?"

His chuckle was vaguely rueful. "What social life? My only interest back then was flying. Every free moment was spent at the airport, working on planes, bugging the seasoned pilots for stories and advice, dreaming of the day I sat behind the controls of a fighter jet."

"So you went into the air force after graduating high school? Or did you attend college first?"

"Air Force Academy," he replied with just a trace of justifiable pride.

"Very impressive," she assured him gravely, managing not to smile at the gleam in his wicked blue eyes. A very impressive man, she decided. No wonder she found him so fascinating. What woman wouldn't? "I'll bet you were a hell-raiser in your Academy days."

He widened his eyes in an effort to look innocent. An effort that failed miserably. "Now whatever made you say that?"

She grimaced expressively. He was probably still a hell-raiser, she thought. He'd certainly played havoc with her routine during the past few days! "I can't imagine," she murmured dryly, making him chuckle as he cut into his meat.

They were nearly finished with the veal scaloppine and stuffed eggplant when Rob startled her by asking, "What about your writing, Sabrina? I always thought you'd be a bestselling author by now."

How in the world had he known about that? She thought of the hours she'd spent in her youth, scribbling love stories into wire-bound notebooks, creating friends she wouldn't have to leave behind when her father got the urge to move again. Her pleasure in writing had gotten her through some rough, lonely years—but had always been her secret. Or so she'd thought, anyway.

"I'm afraid I'm much too busy with my business to concentrate seriously on writing now," she prevaricated, telling herself that she was being at least partially truthful. After all, she found time for her current manuscript only on occasional free evenings or weekend afternoons. She could hardly consider herself a serious writer.

"Don't you ever still dream of being published? Even as a teenager, you were very talented. You won first place in a state-wide short-story contest for high school students, didn't you?"

She cleared her throat, avoiding his eyes. There was something just a bit too intimate about discussing a consuming passion with a virtual stranger. Admitting vague longings that had little chance of being fulfilled made her feel too vulnerable, too open to condescension or, worse, pity.

Maybe someday she'd find the time to finish her book, the nerve to submit it to a publisher. But, in the meantime, she had no intention of sharing that secret dream with anyone else. She knew from bitter experience how others could tarnish one's dreams. "I'm not a starry-eyed adolescent now, Rob. I'm very content with my sensible, profitable career."

Rob frowned. "You make it sound as though you think writing is a less-than-respectable profession."

She shrugged again. "Writing is for dreamers. The odds of being successful at it—or even being published in the first place—are slim. Too chimerical for my tastes."

"You used to be a dreamer, Sabrina," he said quietly, studying her face with what almost appeared to be sadness in his perceptive blue eyes. "What happened to you?"

What had happened to her?

How did she explain her father? The ultimate vagabond. A dreamer who'd spent his entire life chasing after rainbows, hauling his family with him, selfishly putting his desires over his children's security. He'd died when Sabrina was barely seventeen, leaving plenty of debts and no money with which to pay them.

Or her husband. Burt, who'd offered so much and given so little. Who'd taken her fragile dreams of her own home and family and ground them into dust.

"I grew up, Rob," she replied finally, as she had answered that same question on the day they'd met in her office building. "We all have to sometime."

"Maybe." He looked down at his plate, hiding his expression.

"So what about you? Have you changed much since you knew me before?" she inquired lightly, deciding to switch topics.

He chuckled. "You never give up, do you? Here's your dessert."

Sabrina sighed dramatically and dipped her spoon into rich zabaglione served over raspberries. "I hate to think of the calories I've put away tonight."

"You don't look as though you need to count calories." He took the opportunity to admire the slender curves outlined by her clinging emerald dress.

Sabrina had to struggle to keep her color down, chiding herself for reacting like the teenager he claimed to have known instead of an experienced, thirty-three-year-old woman. She knew better than to trust an infatuation based on physical attraction.

Then, because she was basically an honest person, she admitted to herself that her attraction to Rob Davis wasn't entirely physical. She admired his quick wit and the lively humor that danced in his bright blue eyes. The way he listened to her with his complete attention. Few of the men she knew were such good listeners. She couldn't remember the last time she'd talked so much about herself, and yet Rob gave no indication of being bored. She was more than ready to turn the conversation back to him now.

"Just brimming with questions, aren't you, Sunshine?" Rob asked humorously, as if he'd read her mind.

Sunshine? The casually uttered nickname startled her for a moment. And then she remembered that she had quite a few questions for him. "What about your own family? Are your parents still living?"

"Yes."

"Do they live in Irving?" she persisted.

He shook his head. "They moved to Fort Worth several years ago."

"Do you have any brothers or sisters?"

"A sister." He sipped his espresso, answering her questions without giving away more than he wanted her to know.

She scowled. "Have I met her?"

"Yep."

Sabrina placed her own cup on the table with a little thud. "You're not being very helpful!"

"I've answered every question you've asked," he pointed out, his eyes gleaming in appreciation of her frustration. "Feel free to continue."

Amused despite her frustration, as he'd known she would be, of course—the rat—Sabrina sighed and threw up her hands in defeat. "I want to know exactly how we met," she said firmly, deciding she'd never get anywhere with the non-answers he was giving her.

Rob hesitated, considering his response. Sabrina remembered his claim that he never lied, and she could tell that he was trying to formulate an evasive, yet still truthful answer.

"May I bring you anything else, sir?" a courteous waiter asked at Rob's elbow.

His face mirroring his relief, Rob smiled and shook his head. "We'd like the check now, please."

"You're really enjoying this, aren't you?" Sabrina almost growled at him.

He laughed. "You bet. I think you've had your own way for entirely too long, Sabrina Marsh. Don't you think it's time someone challenged you a bit?"

"Someone like you, I suppose?"

He reached out to touch her hand, seeming to send sparks of sensation all the way up her arm. "Someone exactly like me," he replied, the words sounding uncomfortably like a vow.

ROB STARTED THE ENGINE of his car and turned up the radio, looking rather pleased with himself. Sabrina settled back to ride quietly for a while, realizing that Rob now knew a great deal about her, thanks to his unexplained prior knowledge and all the talking she'd done over dinner. And still she knew very little about him.

She knew he was a pilot, that he was extraordinarily attractive, naturally charming and unselfconsciously sexy. And dangerous to her peace of mind. She wasn't used to the feelings he elicited from her and they disturbed her.

She concentrated, instead, on the challenge he'd thrown her, trying very hard to place Rob. *Think, Sabrina. Davis. Irving. Texas.*

Davis. Her eyes widened. There'd been a family living down the street from her—had their name been . . . yes. Davis!

Confident that she was on the right track, she chewed her lower lip as she tried to wade through seventeen years of memories. She hadn't known the family very well, but she had baby-sat for them a time or two. Their children—two, she remembered, a boy and a girl—hadn't been very old, even younger than Colin, who was two years behind Sabrina. But, she dimly recalled, there had been a large extended family—lots of cousins who all lived in the same area. Colin had played ball with them in the empty lot at the end of the street. She didn't specifically remember one named Rob, but by that time, she'd already gotten into the habit of staying somewhat aloof from most of the kids at school. It was easier, that way, to say goodbye when her father got the urge to move on.

So now she knew. It had to be. Rob was a cousin of the Davis children she used to baby-sit. Which explained some of the things he knew about her—but not all. How in the world had he known about her favorite foods? Her favorite color? Her secret hobby of writing? He must have been a good friend of Colin's at the time, she decided, wishing again that her brother was back in town. Colin could have told Rob those things. Though she couldn't for the life of her decide why Rob would have asked. Unless . . .

She slanted him a sideways glance, admiring his profile as he drove with seemingly total concentration. Had he liked her then? If so, she wondered why he hadn't tried to get to know her. Why he hadn't asked her out. She couldn't believe that Rob had ever been shy, even as a teenager.

"What's so funny?" Rob inquired curiously, bringing her back to the present with a start.

She blinked, discovering that he was pulling the car into her driveway. Had she been smiling? "I beg your pardon?"

"You've been so quiet. I was just wondering if your smile had anything to do with me," he explained, killing the engine.

"Could be. Would you like to come in for coffee?" She was determined to find out about him now, and there was always Angel to assist her if Rob seemed unwilling to leave once she'd found out what she wanted to know. Not that she expected any trouble. For some reason, she instinctively knew that Rob could be trusted in some ways. He was no danger to her, physically.

Emotionally—well, that was another story altogether.

"Thanks. I'd like that." He jumped out of the car as if afraid she might change her mind.

"I like your apartment," he commented minutes later, looking around from his kneeling position on the living room carpet. Angel stood beside him, reveling in Rob's attention, wagging his cropped tail as if Rob were an old friend who'd been gone for days.

"Thank you," she replied, waiting for the usual comment about her liberal use of yellow in her decor. When it failed to come, she relaxed. "I'll make the coffee. You can talk to Angel."

"Forgive me for saying this, Brie, but Angel is really a dumb name for a ferocious-looking male Doberman," Rob commented, rising to follow her to the kitchen with the dog at his heels.

"I know." She smiled without offense and reached for the coffee canister. "His sire was a champion registered as Prince of Darkness and his registered name is Archangel Lucifer. I shortened it to Angel when I got him."

"Softened his image, hmm?"

"Only until he narrows those little yellow eyes and bares his fangs," Sabrina answered affectionately.

"I'll bet. I see you have a dog door built into the kitchen door. That must be convenient for you."

"Yes. The O'Neals next door installed one just like it. Angel can go out of this one and into theirs. They adore him, especially their daughter, Mandy." She poured water into the coffeemaker. "Where will you go when your vacation is over, Rob? Where are you stationed?"

"I'm leaving for Germany in a few weeks. I'm tentatively stationed there for two years, depending on further political developments in Europe."

She kept her eyes focused fiercely on the coffeemaker. "Germany," she repeated, her voice rather hollow. "That's very far away—from your family," she added inanely.

It wasn't as if she'd ever expected anything to come from this anyway, she reminded herself somewhat bleakly.

"Yes. I've never been to Germany. I enjoy seeing different parts of the world."

"Ever get homesick?"

"Sometimes," he admitted. "My phone bill usually runs high enough to feed a small family."

She managed the expected smile, then changed the subject. "Are you hungry, Rob? I have some cookies, I think."

"Are you kidding?" he asked with a smile, though she felt him watching her intently. Had he sensed her disappointment with his career? "I may not eat again for days," he said lightly.

"Oh, of course. Me, either," she confessed. So much for reluctantly intriguing mystery dates. The game suddenly lost its appeal. She decided to end it once and for all. "There was a family who lived down the street from mine in Irving. Their name was Davis. You're related to them, aren't you? One of their cousins, perhaps?"

His grin widened. "Think you've got it all figured out, do you? Is that your third guess?"

She nodded, keeping her voice light. "I realized you must be a relative of theirs when I suddenly remembered the family. I used to baby-sit their children, Lizzie and—gosh—what was the little boy's name? Skipper? No, Scooter. He was a cute kid. Do you ever hear from him?"

Rob swallowed hard, but he answered evenly. "Sometimes."

"He was a sickly little thing, as I remember. He was about ten when I knew them, but small for his age. He had asthma, I think. Did he turn out okay?"

Nodding affirmatively, he moved closer to her, propping his strong arms on the counter at either side of her to trap her between them. "Not as okay as you turned out. You were a pretty teenager, Sabrina, but you're a beautiful woman. So beautiful."

She'd been expecting him to kiss her all evening, of course. But she'd thought she'd have more warning. He caught her off-guard when his mouth covered hers, unprepared against the electric response that was becoming all too familiar, all too arousing. She shouldn't respond to Rob this intensely, especially not now when she knew without doubt that there was no future for them. But there didn't seem to be much she could do about it except close her eyes and lose herself in the skillful pleasures of his kiss.

Rob didn't kiss her as though they'd just been out on their first date, as if their lips had only touched briefly a couple of times before. Instead, he kissed her as if they really had known each other for years. As if they'd known each other intimately. His lips moved firmly over hers, and when she automatically parted her lips, he surged inside without hesitation, his tongue finding hers and greeting it hungrily.

She had never been kissed so perfectly. Her mind started to spin at the feel of his body pressed to hers. She grasped the counter behind her in a desperate effort to prevent herself from reaching for him, one last attempt at maintaining control of the evening. Then his hands moved, lifting from the countertop to grasp her arms and gently pull them around his waist.

He lifted his head for a moment to look at her and she stood looking mutely back, her hands remaining where he'd placed them. Her lips trembled with the words she should speak to bring the evening to an end, but no sound escaped them. Her eyes met his. He groaned, raising an unsteady hand to cup the back of her head and hold her still for his next kiss, a gentle, persuasive caress that proved to be her undoing.

Her arms lifting to slide around his neck, Sabrina closed her eyes and tilted her head against his hand to take his kiss more deeply. He accepted the unspoken invitation eagerly, surging into her mouth again and again until she was clinging helplessly to him, kissing him back with a passion that should have astonished her, but somehow didn't.

"Sabrina," Rob rasped, dragging his mouth from hers. "I've either got to leave now or make love with you. I've never wanted anyone this much in my life. Will you ask me to stay?"

She stiffened, common sense returning with a jolt. "Rob, no—I don't—"

"I know you don't," he interrupted, stroking her hair. "I don't usually rush into something like this either. But we're not strangers, you and I. I think we've known each other for an eternity."

She was almost frightened to realize that she felt exactly the same way. Her eyes searched the face that was so new to her and yet already so familiar. She had never before been tempted to make love with a stranger. She was too cautious, too fastidious for one-night stands. On the other hand, she was old enough to grasp at a chance for a night's ecstasy. She knew by instinct that Rob could show her what lovemaking was supposed to be like. Would she be a fool to pass up this chance, or would she be even more foolish to allow him to get that close to her?

"It's happening too fast," she whispered, though her arms had tightened of their own volition around his tautly corded neck.

"I know," he murmured, kissing her temple, her eyelids, her nose, and finally her soft, responsive mouth. "I want you, Sabrina. But I won't push you. I'll go if you tell me to."

"You'd better go."

He stiffened in silent protest, but only for a moment. Then he lifted his hands to remove her arms from around his neck and stepped back. "Good night, Brie. I'll call you tomorrow." He turned toward the living room, patting Angel's head as he passed him.

"Rob!" Sabrina called out, stopping him in his tracks. He turned slowly toward her, his smoky blue eyes flaring with hope.

She stood still, trembling and chewing her lower lip. What was she doing? she asked herself wildly. She had to let him go. Still, the thought of watching him walk out was wrenchingly painful. "Never mind," she murmured finally.

He looked disappointed, but nodded. "Will you see me tomorrow night?"

No. Tell him no, Sabrina. You're only going to be hurt if you let this go on. "I—uh—"

"Please."

Damn. "All right." She'd tell him then that there was no future for them. That she didn't date men who weren't as firmly settled in one place as she was now, she decided. She'd allow herself one more evening with him, and then it was over.

He took a step toward her, as if to kiss her again, then seemed to think better of it. "Good night, Sabrina."

And then he was gone, leaving Sabrina and Angel staring wistfully after him.

ROB MADE IT ALL THE WAY to his car before letting out his breath in a noisy gust. He felt like a teenager again, just discovering the tantalizing mysteries of the opposite sex. Had he ever reacted that quickly, that powerfully to a kiss?

Pushing his hand through his closely cropped hair, he exhaled deeply before starting the car. Frowning, he backed out of the driveway with one last, wistful glance at her door, beginning to wonder if a lingering boyhood infatuation was all he felt for Sabrina Marsh.

And then he shook his head in an effort to rid himself of the dazed sensation left over from their kisses. What else could it be but a powerful physical attraction? he asked himself logically. He'd only known her for a few days—this time, at least. And it wasn't exactly a great time for him to get seriously involved with any woman, particularly one as deeply rooted as Sabrina.

He was already counting the minutes until he saw her again. But it was only sexual attraction, right? Right, he decided, giving a nod to his determined reflection in the rearview mirror. Sure.

And then he snorted in disgust at his own pitiful attempt at self-delusion.

5

SABRINA FOUND HERSELF spending an inordinate amount of time choosing earrings Friday evening. The black? The gold? Then she scolded herself for being silly and defiantly thrust gold posts through the tiny holes in her earlobes. The gold earrings looked fine with the black silk confection she'd donned a few minutes earlier. Rob had called her at work that morning and had asked her for dinner and dancing that evening. She'd agreed very briskly, because she'd already told him she would see him that night, but she told herself that she was not going to fall for his charms this time. She had herself firmly under control again. She hoped.

She smoothed her hair into a sleek French twist, which, combined with her refined makeup and beautifully styled dress, gave her an appearance of competent, slightly daunting sophistication. Not that that image had helped her out the night before, she remembered. But it would tonight. Rob would find out tonight that she'd come a long way from the silly teenager he'd once known. It was past time she regained control of this disconcerting situation.

Her stern control lasted until Rob smiled at her when she opened the door to him. "Lady, you are beautiful," he murmured, looking at her in a way that brought hot color to her cheeks to spoil the cool, implacable look she'd worked so hard to achieve. He didn't kiss her, but he may as well have from the reaction he elicited with just that look.

Without doubt it was the most romantic evening in Sabrina's life. From the exquisite French cuisine at the restaurant where they dined to the smoky glamor of the intimate lounge where they danced, she found herself entertained and charmed by a master. Rob seemed to know by instinct how to entrance her, the way to look at her to make her tremble, the words to say to make her heart beat faster. She tried to remember her earlier resolution to retain control over the evening, but the task proved impossible. No one had ever looked at her this way. No one had ever gone to this much trouble to make her feel special, desired, yet deeply respected.

Even their dancing seemed magically coordinated. Their steps matched beautifully, their bodies molded with intimate perfection. Rob was temptation incarnate, firm body, sexy smile, laughing eyes, caressing words. She was being seduced. She knew it but heaven help her, she thought at one point during the evening, there seemed to be nothing she could do to stop it.

"Tell me about flying, Rob," she urged him when they had taken a moment to rest and sip mixed drinks at a snug little table in a dim corner. "What's it like?"

"I don't think I can describe it to you," he answered slowly. "Not in words that haven't been used too many times before. I was one of those boys who used to watch birds and dream of their freedom. My first flying lesson was everything I had dreamed it would be—and more. I've been a hopeless addict ever since."

"Dreams," she murmured, captured by the word, uncomfortable with the feelings it always aroused in her.

"Yes, dreams," he replied quietly. "I believe in them, Sabrina. I still have them."

"What kind of planes do you fly?" She spoke rapidly, changing the subject.

"Anything that will get off the ground," he answered willingly enough, though his eyes told her he knew what she was doing. "My brother-in-law owns a Cessna 150—a little single-engine two-seater that he encourages me to use when I'm home. That's flying just for the fun of it. But what really turns me on are the fighter jets like the F-15. The power, the speed, the noise, the technology. There's nothing like being right at the edge of the atmosphere with all that power at my fingertips."

"And the danger?" Sabrina asked quietly, trying not to think of all the plane crash descriptions she'd heard and read. Colin had taken her to see *Top Gun* a few years earlier; she still remembered how disturbed she'd been by the scene in which the nice, happy-go-lucky Goose had died in a freak aviation accident. She remembered thinking at the time that the families of such men must possess a great deal of courage to live with the knowledge of the danger their loved ones encountered almost daily.

"It's there," he admitted. "I suppose that's part of the lure, as well," he added rather sheepishly.

"Oh." She couldn't think of anything else to say at the moment. She didn't want him to notice how deeply it bothered her to think of him in peril.

Rob rose suddenly and held out his hand. "Do you hear that music? A true romantic like me can't sit here and listen to that without wanting to dance with you."

Willingly diverted, she stepped into his arms. She wondered if the flying he loved so much could be nearly as beautiful as dancing with him.

Seduction, she thought again, her head cradled in the hollow of his strong shoulder, her hand clasped warmly in his. So this was what it felt like. She found herself as vulnerable to the experience as any other woman, even vaguely reassured that she could still feel things she hadn't felt in so many years. It seemed there was nothing wrong with Sabrina Marsh's hormones, after all.

IT WAS VERY LATE when Rob took her home. She hesitated at the door, knowing she could send him home on the excuse that she had to work in the morning. Knowing somehow that he would accept her excuse without protest. And then she heard herself asking him in.

"Sabrina." He touched her face with fingers that trembled just perceptibly, his voice husky and tender. "I was raised to be a gentleman and I've managed to remain one most of the time, but the feelings you bring out in me aren't very gentlemanly, I'm afraid. I made myself leave you last night when I wanted to take you in my arms and carry you to bed. I don't know if I can be so chivalrous tonight."

He leaned over to rest his forehead against hers, causing her eyelids to drift heavily downward. "I want you so much," he whispered. "I'd better go now while I can."

Sabrina drew in a deep, shuddering breath and tried to think, finding the task incredibly difficult while he was so close. Impossible. It had been so long since she'd done anything just because she wanted to. And she wanted Rob. She'd never wanted anyone the way she wanted this charming, tantalizing stranger—even if it were only for this one night. "Don't go, Rob," she murmured in a voice that couldn't possibly be her own.

He muttered something incoherent and turned his head to kiss her. His mouth closed fiercely over hers, shattering the last of her sanity.

She handed him her key, afraid she'd never be able to control her trembling enough to fit the key to the lock. When was the last time she'd trembled? she wondered fleetingly, staring in bemusement at her hands. She moistened her lips as she stepped inside and patted Angel before turning back to Rob, finding him watching her much too intently.

"Last chance to change your mind," he murmured, trying for a light tone, not quite achieving it.

She smiled and held out her hand. "I'm not changing my mind," she whispered, reveling in the hunger flaring in his blue eyes.

His usually cocky grin wasn't quite steady this time. "Good," he murmured, pulling her into his arms. He kissed her deeply, once, twice, then surprised her by swinging her into his arms, high against his chest, making her laugh and clutch at his shoulders for security. "It's good to hear you laugh," he approved, heading confidently toward the stairs.

It felt good to laugh again. And to ache again in this deliciously wanton way. Her hands caressed the muscles bunching in his upper arms as he held her so easily, then curled around his neck. "You make me feel good, Rob Davis," she told him quietly, honestly.

His eyes gleamed in sensual promise. "I haven't even begun," he assured her. At the base of the stairs he paused and lowered her to her feet. "I'm not Rhett Butler," he murmured, a trace of humor still underlying the passion that deepened his voice. "I wouldn't want to ruin the mood by tumbling downstairs with you."

She took his hand and matched her steps to his, leading him up the stairs to the short hallway onto which the two bedrooms opened. Hers was on the left. They didn't bother with the light when they entered but made their way to the bed by the dim illumination provided by the full moon streaming through sheer yellow curtains. And then Sabrina turned back to Rob, her arms opening in mute invitation.

Rob stepped into Sabrina's arms and lowered his head, his lips moving against hers so lightly that she soon found herself wanting more, needing more, finally demanding more. Her arms went up, around his neck, pulling his head closer. Rob accepted the gesture for what it was, an invitation for him to take control. He immediately took advantage of the opportunity to dazzle her again with his skillful kisses.

Her attention shifted from her marvelously assaulted lips to her breasts, swelling through layers of fabric to press into his solid chest, and to her silk-and-nylon-covered legs, which fit snugly between his longer, harder ones. Her entire body seemed incredibly sensitized, quivering to life in surprising places.

She wasn't aware of making a conscious decision to shift her weight, but she did and he followed her eagerly down to sit beside her on the edge of the bed, his mouth still moving against hers. Sabrina circled his neck with her arms, fingers sliding into the springy, soft hair at the back of his head. She loved his hair, wished he wore it a bit longer. But he couldn't in the air force, she remembered.

And then forgot about anything but the feel of his hand as it slipped downward to cup one breast through the clinging fabric of her dress. Startled by her body's instant response, she stopped kissing him for a moment to concentrate on the sensations he created with his talented fingers. She was aware of a sudden urge to look down and see if she were still wearing clothes. Rob seemed completely unhindered by the layers of cloth as he circled and kneaded her swelling fullness, the heat of his palm penetrating the fabric.

Sabrina pressed herself more fully into his hand, her own moving away from his hair to splay across his broad back. Slowly, savoringly, she slid her palms down the length of his spine, loving the solid, virile feel of him.

Rob found the fastenings at the back of her neck. She felt cool air on her bare shoulders, then lower as the dress opened beneath his fingers. He dropped his head to kiss the delicate line of her shoulder, sliding the garment with tantalizing leisure down her lowered arms to her fingertips. Leaving her hands bound by the sleeves, he stroked the length of her arms from wrist to shoulder and back down before moving to the clasp of her scanty lace bra. And then that, too, was lowered to her wrists and his mouth was on the top curve of her breast, warm and moist and deliciously arousing.

Sabrina wanted to touch him, to unbutton his shirt and feel him against her, but the bunched fabric around her wrists impeded her movements. She tried to free her hands, but he snagged her wrists and stopped her, pressing her backward until she lay beneath him on the bed.

Without giving her time to react, he took advantage of her position to palm her upthrust breasts, cupping the sides and pushing gently inward before burying his face between them. He worshipped her with his breath and lips and teeth and tongue, brushing, rubbing, nipping and licking until Sabrina thought she would scream if he didn't stop teasing her. She arched convulsively upward, crying out breathlessly when he responded by taking one breast deep into his mouth, suckling it thoroughly before repeating the glorious attack on the other.

With a surge of strength, Sabrina jerked her hands from her sleeves and cupped his head between them, the dress gathered heedlessly at her waist. She stroked his face, then pulled at his shoulders, urging him upward, her lips hungry for his. He needed no second invitation, pushing himself forward to cover her body with his, his mouth taking hers with barely restrained force. She held him tightly before reaching impatiently for his tie, fumbling in her fervor.

He tolerated her awkward efforts for a time, then grew impatient and pulled away to rip the tie from his neck in one smooth movement. The buttons on his shirt opened much more easily under his fingers than they would have for hers. And then his hands were at her waist, stripping away her dress and lacy undergarments with careful haste. When he came back to her, his shirt, slacks, socks and briefs had joined the pile of clothing on the floor and Sabrina was finally able to feel the entire length of him against her.

"You feel so good," they moaned in unison, then laughed softly together, their fiery passion undimmed by the intimate humor.

The smile remaining to deepen the corners of her mouth, Sabrina closed her eyes and burrowed into the corded juncture of his neck and shoulder. Ah, he felt so good. He allowed her to indulge herself only for a moment, and then he levered away from her, his hands sweeping her supple length to find the crisp tangle of blond curls between her legs. "So beautiful," he muttered. "So very beautiful."

Sabrina gasped at the sure possessiveness of his touch. He seemed to know just how to please her, just as he'd known how to romance her earlier in the evening. She parted her legs for him, her hands sliding across his smooth chest and down to his flat stomach. His chest was bare, sleek, almost hairless, but there were soft, springy curls beneath his navel. "Ah, yes, Sabrina. Touch me, sweetheart," he groaned, his muscles rippling beneath her palms.

Her hand slipped down to cup him, making him gasp at her touch. Like Rob, she seemed to know where to stroke, what he liked, what made him shudder with pleasure. He retained only enough coherence to make sure that she was protected, and then they both sensed when the moment was right for him to lift himself on his forearms and lower his body between her raised knees.

She felt him pressing against her hidden opening and arched to meet him. "Yes, Rob, yes! Please."

"Sabrina. You want me, don't you, sweetheart?" He paused just before entering her, his voice conveying an unexpected vulnerability.

"Rob." Her hands gripped his back, fingers clenching into his resilient flesh. "Don't you know?"

"I want to hear you say it. Tell me, Brie."

"I want you. I've never wanted anyone like this."

He surged against her, burying himself deeply within her. Sabrina gasped. He stilled instantly. "Did I hurt you?"

She shook her head against the pillow, urging him on with sinuous movements of her hips.

His body arching into a thrilling rhythm, Rob kissed her, his tongue tasting the sounds torn from her throat. Sabrina clung to him, unable even to say his name. As if prompted by his poetic quotes of flying, her mind filled with images. She and Rob flying together, higher and higher, faster and faster toward the sun, finally bursting through the clouds with an ecstatic shout of glorious freedom.

Her body bowed rigidly upward, her knees tightening around his slim hips. As the shudders rocked through her, loosening her hold on him, she collapsed to the bed, amazed that it had taken her so long to find out what lovemaking could really be like.

Rob kissed her again, finding his own fulfillment with a muffled exclamation against her swollen lips.

After a very long time during which the only sounds were pounding hearts and ragged, gradually slowing breathing, Rob twisted to relieve her of his weight, drawing her immediately to his side. Sabrina snuggled into his taut, damp shoulder, eyes closed as she savored the moment, content to be in his arms. Deciding to worry about ramifications later—much later—she allowed herself to drift, slipping easily into a satiated, dreamless sleep.

IT WAS STILL DARK in the room when Sabrina awoke. A blurred glance at the illuminated bedside clock let her know it was only 2:00 a.m. A sheet covered her bare body, which was snuggled intimately against another warm, relaxed form. Her eyes flew fully open as reality hit her. She'd made love with Rob Davis. A man she'd known less than a week. A serviceman who'd be going overseas very soon.

But she didn't regret asking him to stay, she decided, rolling carefully toward the edge of the bed. No woman should live an entire lifetime without finding such enchantment at least once.

Her movements roused Rob and he reached out reflexively to grasp her wrist. "Sabrina?" he asked with that trace of vulnerability she'd detected earlier.

She leaned back down to drop a feather kiss on his cheek. "I just remembered that I left the lights on downstairs."

"I turned them off an hour ago," he informed her, rising on one elbow. The moonlight streaming through the window behind him illuminated him without color, glistening on his broad shoulders, silvering his hair, shadowing his smiling face.

"You did? I didn't hear you get up."

He stroked her arm with the back of his hand, chuckling. "You were sleeping pretty soundly. You didn't even stir when I blundered into your closet looking for the bathroom."

"You needn't sound so smug about it," she accused him indulgently, lying back down beside him.

He laughed. "I wasn't bragging."

"Weren't you?" She reached up to touch his face, enjoying the night-roughened feel of his cheek.

His knuckles lightly grazed the top of one breast, making her shiver in renewed arousal. She wanted him again, she realized with a start. Was her body trying to make up for years of celibacy in one night? Or were her feelings for Rob more than desire, more than the lure of making love with a sexy stranger?

Uncomfortable with the direction her thoughts had taken, she reached up to slide a hand behind his head and kiss him. His lips curved in a pleased smile against hers, then softened to the response she'd craved. The man certainly knew how to kiss.

Rob's hand tightened on her breast, the beading nipple cupped in his warm palm. He kneaded gently, then impatiently swept the sheet away and reached for the bedside lamp. "This time I want to see you," he murmured, his eyes gleaming in the shadows.

Uncomfortable only for a moment in the lamp's soft golden light, Sabrina relaxed when she noted the appreciation on Rob's face as he looked at her. "You're so beautiful," he murmured—and she wanted to believe him.

It had been so long since anyone had looked at her that way, so long since she'd cared whether another person found her attractive. She cared with Rob.

Unable to resist touching him, she trailed her fingertips from the junction of his neck down the arm supporting his weight, subtle muscles bunched beneath the sleek, warm skin. Her breathing shallowed, as her eyes swept him.

She admired the muscular perfection of his chest. Well, not quite perfection. A two-inch long strawberry birthmark lay just below his right nipple, something she hadn't noticed in the darkness before. Her eyes fixed on that birthmark, widening in shock as memory jolted.

An undersized little boy, sitting on a step, shirtless in the hot Texas sun. His blue eyes peering resentfully from be-

neath a shaggy fringe of dark hair, he sat with skinny shoulders hunched forward as he wheezed for breath and watched the other boys wrestle and tumble in the grass. Her young heart twisting in sympathy, a teenaged Sabrina offered him a candy bar, wishing she could do more to ease the hurt the other boys' mockery had caused. The boy looked up and thanked her, his slightly blue-tinged lips curving into an uncommonly sweet smile, his prominently ribbed chest heaving, drawing her eyes to the oddly shaped strawberry birthmark just below his right nipple.

"Oh, my God!" Sabrina breathed, her eyes flying to Rob's suddenly grim features, her hand dropping limply to her side. "I know who you are!"

He inhaled deeply, dark eyebrows contracting. "Don't look so appalled, Sabrina. It doesn't make the least bit of difference."

"No difference? Then why didn't you tell me last night who you are, or the day before that?" she demanded rather shrilly, pushing herself upright, clutching the sheet to her breast. "You let me think it was all a game, challenging me to find out on my own how we'd met. Instead, you lied to me."

"I didn't lie to you. I told you I was related to the Davis family," he pointed out evenly.

Her laugh bordered hysteria. "No, you didn't lie. You just neglected to tell me that you were the little boy I used to baby-sit, didn't you, *Scooter?*"

6

"I MADE EVERYONE stop calling me Scooter when I hit puberty," Rob told her flatly. "My name is Robert Steven Davis. I prefer Rob."

Sabrina felt dazed. Her mind struggled laboriously to cope with this revelation, trying to match the virile, fascinating man who'd made such exquisite love to her with the hazy memory of an undersized, complex little boy.

"Don't look at me like that, Sabrina," he snapped irritably, shifting to sit beside her, unconcerned that she'd grabbed the sheet and left him uncovered. "Dammit, that's why I didn't tell you before. I wanted you to accept me as the man I am, not the boy I used to be."

"How old *are* you?" She steeled herself for his answer, unable to remember exactly how much younger he was.

"I'm twenty-eight. And, yes, I know you're thirty-three, but I couldn't care less. My attraction to you has nothing to do with the year you were born. I would hope you feel the same way about me."

"Twenty-eight," she murmured as if she hadn't heard anything else. That suddenly sounded so young. She hadn't dated anyone under thirty since her divorce. Rob was right, in a way. The small age difference shouldn't matter, especially since there was no future for them, anyway.

But for some reason it did. There'd been a tantalizing excitement in making love with a dashing pilot, indulging her long-ignored physical needs with a man straight out of most women's fantasies. But now she found herself vaguely shocked that she'd been to bed with the little boy from down the street years earlier, the child she'd baby-sat for a dollar an hour while his parents went out for an evening.

"Dammit, Sabrina," Rob growled, his frown leveling at the death-grip she maintained on the sheet she held to her chin. "I'm not that young. Surely you're not still thinking of me as a boy."

His words brought her abruptly back to the present. A boy? Her eyes swept the mature nude body poised tensely on the bed, still in a state of semi-arousal from their interrupted lovemaking. She laughed shortly. "No, Rob. I know you're not a boy."

"I'm a man. Not some little kid called Scooter," he reiterated deliberately.

"Yes! But you didn't have to take me to bed to convince me of that. I have eyes."

"Would you have had dinner with me if I'd introduced myself as Scooter Davis?"

"Probably," she admitted.

"Would you have made love with me?"

Sabrina bit her lip. Would she have? His seductive magnetism had all too easily overcome her scruples about going to bed with him on such short acquaintance, though she'd resisted other temptation for years. Temptation? Hah! She'd never even *known* temptation until Rob Davis had strolled into her life. Still, would her attraction to him have overcome those awkward memories? "I don't know."

He eyed her broodingly. "You would have," he announced finally. "It might have taken a bit longer, but the outcome was inevitable."

He reached for her as if to prove his point. Instinctively, she flinched away from his touch. His eyes widened, his hands dropping. She'd hurt him, she thought in quick regret. She hadn't really known she could.

"I'm sorry—I—" She stopped and bit her lower lip, wondering what else to say. Hating the awkwardness that had suddenly developed between them.

"You want me to leave?" He asked the question with little expression, his eyes shuttered now.

"Maybe you should," Sabrina agreed quietly, not quite meeting his eyes. "We're both tired and...well—" What else could she say? She was still too preoccupied with her discovery of Rob's identity to think clearly.

Little "Scooter" Davis. Oh, heavens.

Rob only nodded. "All right. I'll give you a call tomorrow."

"Fine." She couldn't resist watching through her lashes as he stood and reached unselfconsciously for his clothes. Definitely not a boy, she thought again, eyes lingering on the taut sculpting of his back and buttocks. If only they hadn't known each other before under such awkward circumstances. If only he wasn't in the service, just passing through on his way to a foreign assignment. If only she really was the type to indulge in a brief, passionate fling without fear of becoming too deeply involved. If only...

Her wistful thoughts were interrupted when he leaned over the bed and placed a firm, almost challenging kiss on her still-tender lips. "I'll talk to you tomorrow. Good night, Sabrina."

"Good night, Rob," she whispered. She wondered if she should be saying goodbye, instead.

"YOU LOOK LIKE HELL."

Rob winced and slid into a chair at his sister's table, ducking his head to avoid her frank, intense scrutiny. "Pass the coffee, would you?"

She poured him a cup from the insulated carafe in front of her and slid it across the table. "Looks like you need it."

"I didn't sleep too well last night," he admitted, sipping the strong, hot brew with a sigh of pleasure.

"Maybe because you didn't get in until dawn?" Liz suggested sweetly.

He scowled. "I was in before dawn."

"Three o'clock, Rob. I heard you."

"What were you doing up at three o'clock?"

She patted her stomach with a deep sigh. "Junior, here, isn't much of a sleeper. He likes to kick and play during the night, which makes it hard for me to get much sleep."

"Oh." He reached for the covered dish sitting by his plate, lifting the lid to find still-warm scrambled eggs, bacon and a bran muffin the housekeeper had prepared for him. "This looks good."

Liz popped a bit of muffin into her mouth, swallowed, then cocked her head in characteristic curiosity. "Well?"

He concentrated on spreading butter on his own muffin. "Well, what?"

"Are you going to tell me what you were doing until three o'clock?"

"No."

"Come on, Rob, what's going on between you and Sabrina Marsh? You've been out with her two nights in a row now, you spent most of yesterday smiling to yourself, and this morning you look like you spent a long, hard night on the bricks. Naturally I'm curious."

"You were born curious," Rob accused, smiling a little at her understatement. "And you never paid any attention to the parable of the nosey cat."

Liz sighed. "You're not going to tell me anything, are you?"

"Probably not." He bit neatly into a slice of bacon.

Some people would have given up at that point. Not Liz. "Did you tell her how she knew you before?"

He swallowed and answered resignedly. "She knows."

"How'd she react?"

He shrugged. "She wasn't overjoyed."

Liz tried unsuccessfully to swallow a giggle. At Rob's quick frown, she spread her hands conciliatorily. "Well, it's funny, Rob. I can imagine how *I* would feel if one of the little boys I used to baby-sit suddenly turned up as a good-looking man and started making passes at me."

Rob started to protest her description of his behavior, then found himself intrigued by her words. "How *would* you feel?" he asked seriously.

Liz sighed again. "Old."

"That's ridiculous. You're twenty-six. Sabrina's only thirty-three and doesn't look that."

Shaking her head, Liz smiled as she tried to make him understand. "Rob, think about it. This woman used to insist that you finish your milk at dinner. She ordered you to brush your teeth before sending you off to bed at nine o'clock. She sent us to our rooms when we fought over the rules of our board games when you were ten and I was eight. You don't really think she can just forget about that now that you've appeared all grown up and gorgeous, do you?"

Scowling, Rob stirred his scrambled eggs with his fork, appetite fading. "That's ridiculous," he repeated in a mutter. Still, he wondered if Liz was right.

"Maybe so. But whoever said women had to be logical?"

He snorted. "If I'd said that, you'd have called me sexist."

Liz grinned cheerfully. "Yep. We reserve the right to make fun of our own gender. And yours."

But Rob was still considering his sister's suggestion about Sabrina's emotions. He found it hard to truly believe he made Sabrina feel old. After the way he'd responded to her last night? No way. He'd simply startled her, perhaps embarrassed her a bit with her discovery.

Knowing what he did about Sabrina, she'd dislike feeling awkward and out of control. He'd simply have to help her get past those feelings. Because he had no intention of leaving Dallas without tasting again the passion that had flared so hotly, so gloriously between them. He'd never experienced anything as powerful as their lovemaking last night. It had been more than just physical, more than mere desire. He'd wanted her as he'd never wanted another woman, and that hunger wasn't in the least abated by the satisfaction of their one night together. He'd spent the remainder of the night staring at the ceiling in his sister's guest bedroom, replaying the sensual memories, trying without success to analyze what had made the experience so different from anything he'd known before.

Who'd have thought, he wondered almost dispassionately, that he'd have fallen this hard, this fast? And what the hell was he supposed to do now?

"Rob . . . you're not getting in over your head here, are you?" Liz asked carefully when the silence had stretched noticeably.

He looked up cautiously. "What do you mean?"

"Well, you have to admit that you have a tendency to jump in feet first whenever you find something you want. The way you did with flying, with the air force, with that poor girl you scared half to death a few years ago when you decided it was time to have a 'serious relationship' because you'd never had one before. She took to her heels, as I remember."

Why had he come back to Liz's house last night, Rob asked himself with an inward moan. Why hadn't he driven on into Fort Worth and stayed with his parents even though he'd known Liz had expected him? At least they wouldn't have given him the third degree over breakfast, or reminded him of events in his past that were better forgotten. If only Gordon weren't working overtime to clear his schedule so he could take time off with his wife when the baby was born. Gordon could have deflected some of Liz's attention from her brother's social life.

Not knowing what else to say, he fell back on a sometimes-successful sibling retort. "Shut up, Liz."

She laughed. "All right. I can take a hint. Just be careful, will you? I mean, you're leaving in three weeks. I'd hate to see you get hurt before you go."

She wasn't the only one. To reassure Liz—and maybe himself, as well—Rob spoke with airy confidence. "Don't worry about it, Liz. I'm fully aware that there's not time to start anything serious here. I doubt that Sabrina would be interested, anyway. I just enjoy her company, okay? I can spend time with her during the next few weeks without getting too involved."

He crossed his fingers beneath the table as he spoke.

Liz eyed him skeptically for a moment, then squirmed in her chair and pressed a hand to her side. "Damn," she muttered, distracted. "That was a good kick. Your nephew is going to make a great soccer player, Rob."

Relieved, he jumped onto the new subject eagerly, diverting the conversation to the baby, a topic always guaranteed to capture Liz's attention. He was moderately successful at hiding the fact that his own thoughts still centered on Sabrina.

SABRINA FOCUSED on the half-filled page in the typewriter in front of her with single-minded determination, forcing herself to think of her story rather than the night before. At least she had some control over the actions of her characters, or, rather, she had until today. Until her heroine had

totally surprised her by jumping straight into bed with the
black-haired, blue-eyed man who'd suddenly appeared in
the tale.

Chewing her lower lip, Sabrina wondered how to describe the poor, bemused heroine's morning-after feelings.
Shock? Dismay? Self-recrimination? A deep, insidious
craving to do it again?

Slamming her palms down on the desk, Sabrina muttered a savage curse beneath her breath, causing Angel to
look up in startled question from his resting place at her feet.
"What has that man done to me?" she asked herself in a disgruntled mutter. "I'm acting like an infatuated adolescent."

"Which only goes to show," she told her dog firmly, "that
one should never trust a handsome, mysterious pilot with
a to-die-for smile and a body that should be outlawed. Before you know it, he's sneaking into your books—and your
bed," she added with a sigh.

The telephone ring interrupted whatever response Angel
might have made. Catching her breath, Sabrina stared at
the cordless phone beside her typewriter. She knew whose
voice she'd hear when she answered. "Hello?"

"Hi."

She'd guessed correctly. There was no way she could
mistake the deep, rich voice. "Hi, Rob."

"Have you forgiven me yet?"

"For—uh—for what?" she stalled, moistening her lips.

"For turning out to be a bad memory from your past." He
sounded faintly amused.

Reacting rather defensively to his teasing, Sabrina
frowned. "I never said you were a bad memory."

"Then there's no reason you shouldn't have dinner with
me tonight, is there?"

No reason? There were many reasons. It still bothered her that he was five years younger. She was justifiably concerned about becoming too deeply involved with a man who'd be shipping out in a matter of weeks. She wasn't pleased with the thought that she might be his version of "a girl in every port." And, worse, she had a sneaking suspicion that the evening would end exactly the way the previous evening had ended. In bed.

She tried to think of a plausible excuse with a mind that had suddenly gone dysfunctional. "I—uh—"

"Please?"

Oh, hell, what could it hurt to have dinner with him? she asked herself abruptly. She was a grown, responsible woman. She'd end up in bed with him only if she chose to do so—and she'd decide about that later. "All right. Dinner."

"Great." He sounded genuinely pleased. "I'll pick you up at three-thirty, okay?"

"Fine. I'll . . . Wait at minute. Did you say three-thirty?"

"Yeah. Three hours from now. That's plenty of time for you to get ready, isn't it?"

Would she ever understand this man? "You want to go out to dinner at three-thirty in the afternoon?"

"I have a surprise planned. Trust me, okay?"

"Said the smiling shark to the poor little fish," Sabrina muttered, shaking her head.

He laughed. "What was that again?"

"Never mind. I'll see you at three-thirty, Rob. By the way, what should I wear for this surprise of yours?"

"Doesn't matter. You'll look gorgeous whatever you wear. See you, Brie. And thanks."

She listened to the dial tone for a moment, then turned it off. Looking ruefully down at her pet, she slowly shook her head. "The man is insane, Angel. Certifiably. And, worse, I'm beginning to believe it's contagious."

Angel snuffled sympathetically and laid his noble head on her knee. Sabrina turned off her typewriter, knowing she'd get no more writing done that afternoon.

THE DOORBELL RANG at precisely 3:30. How terribly military of him to be so punctual, Sabrina thought with an attempt at humor as she automatically straightened the full skirt of her deep purple shirtwaist dress. She fingered the amethyst pendant resting in the deep V of the neckline as she took a deep breath and pasted on the casual, uninvolved smile she'd decided to greet him with.

Her necklace matched the gold and amethyst earrings peeking out beneath the clouds of blond hair she'd allowed to fall in a tumble of curls to her collar. She rarely wore her hair down; it had been merely a whim to do so today, she assured herself. It had nothing to do with her memories of Rob stroking his fingers through her hair, murmuring how beautiful he thought it was.

Shoving that errant thought from her mind, she opened the door. Her smile wavered at her first sight of him, so dangerously attractive in a brown-and-tan-striped sport shirt, tan pleated slacks and a brown leather bomber jacket. He was wearing his aviator glasses again. She wondered if he knew how sexy he looked in them. She cleared her throat. "Hi."

He leaned over to brush a kiss across her lips. "Hi. You look gorgeous. Just as I said you would."

"Um—thank you." The words came out just a bit breathlessly. How could that mere hint of a kiss turn her into oatmeal after everything they'd done the night before? she wondered almost despairingly. "Would you like to come in?"

He pushed his hands into his pockets, remaining where he stood on the porch. "No, I think we'd better just go, if you're ready."

Without an explanation, Sabrina sensed that he didn't quite trust himself alone inside with her. With the way her pulse was racing just then, she could certainly understand. Snatching up the purse that matched her black flats, she patted Angel and joined Rob outside. "I'm ready."

Sabrina was the one who felt it necessary to make conversation as Rob guided the car away from the house. "How's your sister—Lizzie, isn't it? Does she live here in Dallas?"

"Liz," Rob corrected. "She dropped Lizzie at about the same time I stopped answering to Scooter. Yes, she does live in Dallas, her husband's Gordon Holley, an assistant D.A. And she's fine. Very pregnant, but fine."

"Is this their first baby?"

"Yeah. She and Gordon have been married for a couple of years and they decided it was time to do their part toward propagating the species."

"When's the baby due?"

"Within the next few weeks. She's pretty much housebound now. Gordon's been working long hours trying to clear time off for after the kid's born so I've been running errands for her while I've got time on my hands. That's what I was doing in your office building the other day. Her accountant has his offices there."

"Quite a coincidence," Sabrina murmured.

He slanted her a smile. "A very nice one."

Oh, that smile. Determinedly, she kept the conversation away from their ambiguous relationship. "How do you feel about becoming an uncle?"

His smile deepened. "I'm looking forward to it. It amuses me to think of Liz as a mom, but I'm sure she'll be a natural.

I've been trying to talk her into having the kid while I'm home to see it."

Sabrina chuckled. "I'm sure she's trying to comply."

Rob faked a frown. "Couldn't prove it by me. I ask her every few minutes if she's in labor yet. She gets kind of testy about it after a while."

Sabrina thought that Liz was probably delighted to have her brother out of the house for a few hours. She glanced out the window, then back at Rob. "Where are we going?"

His grin was pure devilment. "You'll see."

Trust me, he'd said. Uh-huh. Sure she would. She took a tighter grip on her purse and carefully watched the route he took. "Does Liz know you've been seeing me?" she heard herself saying. She really hadn't meant to ask that.

"Yeah. I told her the day we ran into each other. She remembers you well, of course. Mom still has a picture of you and your brother with me and Liz. It was taken at a neighborhood picnic, I think. You're wearing a pair of shorts and a swingy little top and I'm standing beside you, salivating over your long, tanned legs."

Sabrina blushed. "You were not," she muttered. "You were just a kid."

"A kid with a major crush on you," he confessed wryly, looking quickly over at her as if to judge her reaction. "Didn't you know?"

She had, as a matter of fact. She simply hadn't expected him to admit it. Remembering the candy bars he'd left on her doorstep, the time he'd challenged her brother to a fight, the time he'd skinned both knees trying to impress her by doing a handstand, she bit her lip against a smile. Her eyes lingered on his muscular thighs, encased so tightly in the twill slacks covering them, then rose slowly up the length of his powerful arms to the broad shoulders and solid chest that had so delighted her the night before. "It's hard to believe you were such a small, sickly child. Whatever happened to your asthma?"

"I outgrew it when I went through puberty," he answered with a shrug. "I spent the next few years lifting weights and playing sports to build up my physique."

"You did a great job of it," she murmured impulsively, then fought down another blush.

His smile was blinding, endearingly cocky. "Why, thank you very much. Could we talk about something else now?"

Her brow lifted in question. "Why? Does it make you uncomfortable to talk about that year in Irving?" Could it possibly bother him as much as it did her?

He hesitated fractionally, then nodded. "I guess so. I'm not thrilled about you thinking of a scrawny, wheezing kid when you look at me."

"Rob, have you looked in a mirror in the past ten years or so?" Sabrina asked dryly.

"Then it doesn't bother you anymore—who I am, I mean?" He sounded oddly hopeful. "You were upset when you first realized it last night."

"It still boggles my mind a bit," she confessed. "But I suppose we have to be able to talk about it."

He nodded. "Looks like we're both a bit touchy about our shared past."

He was right, of course. Sabrina was no more pleased at being remembered as the older blonde he'd platonically admired than he was at having once been a sickly child in her care. So maybe they should forget the past and concentrate on—what? The future? Hardly. There was no future for them beyond the next two and a half weeks, perhaps beyond today. They had only the immediate present.

She decided to allow herself to be content with that.

"Rob, where are you taking me?" she demanded, staring out the window again. "You aren't actually planning to have dinner at Love Field, are you?"

He laughed. "You and that lively curiosity. You remind me of Liz."

Before she could respond to that, he turned into the airport. "Are we, by any chance, going up in a plane?" she asked, already anticipating his answer.

"You guessed it," he agreed cheerfully. "I'd like to show you what I do best."

Sabrina surprised both of them by answering without a beat. "I thought you'd already done that."

His delighted laughter made a thrill of pleasure curl warmly in her stomach. "Lady, you are good for my ego," he told her, reaching over to stroke his knuckles down her left cheek.

Rather pleased with herself for making him laugh, Sabrina covered his hand with hers. She had every intention of enjoying the present immensely.

7

SABRINA HADN'T REALLY expected Rob's brother-in-law's plane to be quite so small. It wasn't even as big as her car. "You're—uh—you're sure that thing's safe?" she asked, staring warily at the red-and-white high-wing.

"Absolutely. Haven't you ever been up in a two-seater?"

"I've never been in any small plane," she confessed. "Only the big commercial airliners."

"Then you're in for a treat," he assured her with suspicious enthusiasm.

"Uh-huh." She watched him circle the plane, performing mysterious rituals she assumed had something to do with safety. "So where will we be going in this glorified kite?"

"Galveston," he replied casually, opening the passenger door for her and holding out his hand.

She stared at him without moving. "Galveston?" she repeated incredulously. "Rob, that's half the state away!"

"Yep. It's just under a three-hour flight, so we'd better get in the air if we want to get home at a reasonable hour."

"Why do you want to have dinner in Galveston?" she asked, hands on her hips.

He only smiled. "You love seafood, right? Tonight we're having fresh seafood. I only wish we had a plane with a little more speed and power available. I'd take you to San Francisco. Ever been there?"

"No," she admitted, allowing him to catch her hand and tug her toward the plane.

"It's great. We'll have to go sometime."

Oh, yeah? When? she wanted to ask. She held her skirt out of the way as he closed the door after helping her into the passenger seat.

"Seat belt," he announced, climbing behind the wheel— or the yoke, as he called it.

"Yes, Captain." She snapped the heavy metal buckle. "Now what?"

Scanning a laminated checklist, he grinned. "You could try closing your eyes and praying."

"I'd already decided to do that, thank you," she replied sweetly, then clenched her fingers around her purse when he started the noisy engine. "Oh, heavens."

Rob laughed, slid a hand behind her head and pulled her to him for a long, thorough kiss. "Trust me, Brie," he murmured when he released her.

She melted back into her seat, her rapid breathing and pounding pulse having absolutely nothing to do with fear of flying.

It took only a matter of minutes after takeoff for Sabrina to realize that she was seeing Rob in his natural element. He looked totally at ease behind the controls of the little plane, very much the handsome pilot in his leather jacket and aviator glasses, his face glowing with the joy of being in the air. It wasn't at all hard to imagine him in the cockpit of a macho military machine. As she watched him, the last of her nervousness dissipated. Rob knew what he was doing. She was safe with him.

And then he gave her that pure-devil grin, yelled "Hang on," twisted the yoke, kicked the rudder and sent the agile little plane into a perfect barrel roll.

"Rob!" Sabrina gasped in outrage when the world had stopped spinning around her, her hands still clasped on the edges of her seat. "You do that again and I'm out of here."

He laughed. "Does that mean you don't want to do loops?"

"No, I don't want to do loops. I'd like to make this trip in a straight, upright path. Got that?"

Still laughing, he nodded. "Yes, ma'am. I hear you."

Watching him, she shook her head in half-amused exasperation. "You really love this, don't you?" she asked, raising her voice to be heard above the noisy engine.

His smile faded when he looked back at her. "This is what I am," he said simply.

Her heart gave an odd little twist. Yes, this is what he was. A pilot. A man who loved traveling, taking chances, reaching for the stars.

A man who had no place in her carefully planned, firmly rooted life.

As if sensing her momentary sadness, Rob set out to entertain her with stories of his aviation career, beginning with the time he'd gotten lost on his first solo by following the wrong highway for his course. He made her laugh, and then made her laugh again and again with other funny tales, some of which she suspected were embellished for her benefit.

The flight passed with unbelievable swiftness. Rob even talked her into taking the controls for a time, giving her a clearly explained, abbreviated flying lesson. He assured her she showed natural talent for flying. She didn't know whether to believe him or not, but she basked in his praise, anyway, proving once again that her head and her emotions were totally out of sync where this man was concerned.

HER HAND CLASPED firmly in Rob's, Sabrina matched her steps to his, breathing in the salty scent of the air as they walked along the seawall after dinner. It was too early for peak tourist season on the popular island of Galveston, so the walks weren't crowded, allowing Sabrina and Rob to stroll at their leisure, talking quietly as they enjoyed the beautiful spring evening.

Rob paused and released her hand long enough to pull off his leather jacket. "Here," he said, draping it around her shoulders to shield her from the chill in the gulf-swept breeze. "It's getting cool."

She snuggled into the jacket, feeling warmly engulfed by the oversize garment that smelled faintly of Rob's citrusy after-shave. She couldn't have asked for a more thoughtful, considerate date. Mrs. Davis had done an admirable job drilling manners into her son, she thought with a reminiscent smile. Their dinner had been wonderful, the conversation easy and fascinating. She'd enjoyed every minute of it. "It's been a lovely evening, Rob."

He turned her into his arms. "The evening's not over yet," he murmured, then lowered his head to kiss her lingeringly.

He was doing it again, she thought dazedly. Weaving his own magical seduction until she could no longer think logically or cautiously, couldn't remember all the reasons she shouldn't get involved with him. Could only want him with every fiber of her feminine being.

Rob bought her an unabashedly tacky little souvenir—a funny little man made of seashells, in one of the many gift shops lining the seawall. "Made from shells collected on this very beach," he assured her gravely, pressing the souvenir into her hand. "Every time you look at it, you'll remember our perfect evening in Galveston."

She turned the figure over and studied the tiny gold sticker that read Made in Korea. "I love it," she assured him with a smile that earned her another kiss.

And then it was time to leave. Sabrina permitted herself one last look around the Galveston airport before climbing into the fueled-and-ready Cessna. She felt almost as if she were leaving a fantasy world on a return trip to reality.

"It's nice up here at night, isn't it?" Rob asked when they'd been flying for nearly half an hour in silence.

Drawing her eyes from the myriad of tiny lights beneath them, Sabrina nodded. "It's beautiful."

Despite the noisiness of the small plane, there was an odd peacefulness in being alone in the air with Rob, the whole state of Texas seemingly spread beneath them like a diamond-studded black velvet blanket. The three-hour trip seemed all too brief. Reality all too near.

IT WAS JUST AFTER midnight when they stood before Sabrina's door, her key in her hand as she looked up at Rob, unwilling for the evening to end quite yet. "Want a cup of coffee before you go?" she asked, not certain whether she should want him to accept or refuse. Knowing that deep down inside she wanted him to stay.

He hesitated. "It's late. Aren't you tired?"

"No," she answered with complete honesty. "Are you?"

He shook his head. "I'd love a cup of coffee. Thanks."

With a somewhat less-than-certain smile, Sabrina unlocked the door.

Fifteen minutes later she carefully carried a tray holding two steaming cups of coffee from the kitchen to the living room. Rob had turned on the stereo and the strains of an all-love-song program played quietly in the background as he sat on the floor by the couch, Angel's head propped on his knee. "My dog adores you, you know," she said conversationally, setting the tray on the coffee table.

"Well, that's half the battle won," Rob replied obscurely, reaching for his cup. He took a sip and closed his eyes in appreciation. "This is good." And then he patted the carpet beside him. "Join me?"

He'd draped his jacket over a chair and kicked off his shoes. Sabrina left her own shoes sitting beside his as she dropped down beside him, her legs curled beneath her full skirt. They sat in comfortable silence for a while, enjoying the music together. It was a very cozy, very intimate, very domestic scene. And for some inexplicable reason, it made Sabrina want to cry.

She sipped her coffee and tried not to think about how Rob would soon be gone from her life as abruptly as he'd become a part of it.

He was the one to speak first, his question totally unexpected. "Did you love him?"

Frowning slightly, she had to think a minute. "You mean, did I love my husband?"

"Yes."

"I've wondered that myself in the years since the divorce," she admitted. "At first, I was very much infatuated with him. When he asked me to marry him, I thought I'd finally found someone who'd always be there for me, someone I wouldn't have to say goodbye to, someone who would want to make a home with me. I'd always wanted a home so badly."

Rob kept his eyes on the dog he was slowly stroking. "And he didn't?"

"No. He wanted to be a football superstar. A hero. He spent the entire five years of our marriage pretending to be just that. I've never been sure exactly why he married me. He never really acted married."

"Where is he now?"

"He's a sportscaster for a small cable television channel in Nebraska. He married a cheerleader for the last team he played for, two years after he and I were divorced."

"Does that bother you—to think of him married to someone else?" Rob's voice was still studiedly casual, his face averted from her.

"No," she answered with complete candor. "It bothered me when he was unfaithful while we were married. Since the divorce, I don't care what he does or who he does it with. If what I felt for him was ever love, it died even before the marriage ended."

"Has there been anyone else since the divorce? Anyone serious, I mean."

She thought of Paul. "There was a man three years later. He was also divorced. We had a great deal in common. I wasn't in love with him, not in the traditional sense, but I thought we had a chance to form a lasting, satisfactory relationship."

"What happened?"

Her smile was not an amused one. "He got a promotion, started taking lots of business trips. Turned out he enjoyed living on the road. He broke it off with me because he said he wasn't ready to settle down again. He was just beginning to live, he said. Different towns, different women. It all went straight to his head. I haven't heard from him since."

"No wonder you're so wary of becoming involved with anyone."

"I haven't had a great deal of luck with romance," she agreed evenly, setting her empty coffee cup on the end table at her elbow.

He stared down into his own cup. "I'd hardly be the type of man you'd want to become involved with either, would I? Obviously my career involves a great deal of travel, a series of moves."

"Another nomad." She tried to keep her voice light. "But it really doesn't matter for us, does it, Rob? After all, we've simply enjoyed a few nice evenings together. We've known from the beginning that there's nothing more to it than that."

A muscle jerked in his firm jaw. "Have we?"

Her throat felt tight. She cleared it. "Yes. We have."

His mouth twisted in a grim smile that was very different from the open, bright grins he usually wore. His voice was somewhat gritty when he spoke, setting his coffee cup out of the way. "If all we have is a temporary affair, then we shouldn't waste any time, should we?"

Before she could anticipate his move, he snagged her wrist and pulled her to him. Angel tactfully left the room in search of his dinner bowl.

"Rob!" Sabrina protested, laughing as she tried to straighten her disheveled clothing.

But he was already lifting her into his arms, holding her so that they were kneeling, her breasts crushed against his chest as he pulled her tightly against him. "I've been wanting you all evening. So badly I wasn't sure I could even wait until we were alone," he muttered, his mouth hovering over hers.

He kissed her with such all-consuming passion that Sabrina moaned, her own tenuous control shattering. Rob's hands were all over her, molding her, arousing her. For the first time she realized exactly why this man could make her respond as no one before. Not her husband, not Paul. No one but Rob.

Other men had wanted her physically, but none of them had really *needed* her. Rob wanted—needed—her with a hunger that was more than physical. He told her with his beautiful eyes, his powerful body, his mind-spinning kisses. It wasn't just a woman he wanted tonight; he wanted Sabrina. She was helpless to resist him. How could she, when she needed him just as badly?

She wanted him. The words floated on shimmering, musical notes through her mind like echoes of the love songs playing in the background as Rob unbuttoned her dress to the waist and eased his hands into the opening. Awkward memories were forgotten in the heat, the passion of his caresses. Sabrina was aware of nothing but Rob, the man who so easily aroused her to a fever pitch of arousal.

The front clasp of her bra seemed to dissolve at the first touch of his fingers. Easing the dress over her shoulders, he lowered his mouth to her exposed breasts. Her fingers spearing into his hair, Sabrina closed her eyes and arched into the hot depths of his mouth, her entire body going soft and liquid.

She'd been infatuated. She'd been intrigued. But she'd never wanted anyone the way she wanted Rob.

He lifted his head from her damp, throbbing breasts to stare down into her face with smoldering eyes. "Tell me you want me."

Her eyes locked with his. "I want you." Reaching upward, she nuzzled her cheek against his rougher one. "I want you." She kissed his chin, then ran the tip of her tongue across his lower lip. "I want you."

He groaned his pleasure with her words and actions. "Show me how much."

Pulling her arms from the sleeves of her unfastened dress, she tossed her bra aside and reached for the buttons of his striped shirt. They opened easily for her. She spread her palms across his solid chest before sliding one hand down to his belt buckle. Her gaze still holding his, she slowly lowered his zipper and slipped her hand inside. Rob gasped and crushed her mouth beneath his.

Smiling against his lips, she stroked him until he trembled against her. He lowered his head to her breast again. She arched back to allow him better access, her hands sliding around to cup his taut buttocks beneath his loosened slacks. Circling one tightly puckered nipple with his tongue, Rob slid his hands up her thighs, lifting her full skirt to her waist as he filled his hands with her, his fingertips sinking into her soft flesh through the thin satin barrier of her panties.

Suddenly impatient, Sabrina levered away from him enough to spread his unbuttoned shirt out of the way. Taking him by surprise, she pushed him onto his back on the carpet, avidly running her hands over his tanned, muscular chest. Leaning over him, she brushed her lips across his flat brown nipples, circling them teasingly with her tongue before attacking sensuously with her lips and the edge of her teeth. Rob drew in a sharp breath, a tremor running through him. His response aroused her even further, burning away any remaining inhibitions.

She eased herself down his body, pushing his slacks downward until they lay recklessly abandoned beside him, along with his briefs. He lay before her, taut and hard and trembling with his need for her, his cheeks flushed with passion, eyes blazing into her. She dropped a kiss on the strawberry birthmark beneath his breast before nibbling a trail to his rock-hard stomach. The tip of her tongue circled his navel, then dipped into it.

Rob moaned, his hands clenching into fists at his sides. He quivered with the restraint he was exerting, but allowed her the freedom to explore him, seeming to sense that she needed to regain some control in their tumultuous, ambiguous relationship. He shuddered when her teeth sank gently into the inside of his thigh. "Ah, Sabrina." His voice was nearly unrecognizable.

She glanced up to see that his eyes had closed, his face glistening with perspiration. And then she moved her mouth inward, nibbling and licking and caressing until he exploded into action, all control gone. Struggling back to his knees, he stripped away her panties, grasped her hips beneath her bunched skirt and pulled her to him, spreading her thighs over his. She pressed her mouth to his and lowered herself onto him, taking him deeply within her.

Rob arched convulsively upward, his fingers biting into her buttocks as he guided her into a rhythm that drove them both to madness. Her hands clenching his shoulders beneath his open shirt, Sabrina leaned backward, her eyes closed, facial muscles clenched. His mouth closed again over the tip of one breast and she cried out, her blood burning in her veins, pulse pounding in her ears. She was dimly aware that the top of her dress was draped behind her, the skirt gathered at her waist, that Rob still wore his shirt. Their half-dressed state only made the act seem somehow sexier, more wicked. She moved wildly with him until the explosion took her, a hoarse cry escaping her as she stiffened in his arms. Rob's grip tightened on her hips as his own violent spasms overtook him.

And then they fell to the carpet, exhausted, arms, legs and items of clothing all tangled together. Burrowing into Rob's sweat-slick shoulder, Sabrina closed her eyes and wished she could freeze time forever to this one, perfect moment.

SABRINA STIRRED on the pillow, slowly coming to the realization that she was naked beneath the sheets. And that, for the second time in three days, she'd taken Rob Davis to her bed. She opened her eyes.

Propped on one elbow, illuminated by the sunlight that indicated the morning was well under way, Rob smiled down at her, obviously enjoying her waking-up disorientation. "Good morning."

She remembered the uninhibited lovemaking on the floor downstairs, the hand-in-hand walk up the stairs to her bedroom, the slow, lingering lovemaking afterward. Trying not to blush, she pushed her hair out of her face. "Good morning. What time is it?"

"Nearly eleven." His hand sliding up her bare side, he nuzzled her neck. "Did anyone ever tell you you're beautiful in the morning?"

"It's been a while," she murmured huskily, stirring beneath his touch.

His lips touched her earlobe. "Are you a good cook?"

Startled into a breathless laugh, she caught his hand just as it would have closed on one breast. "Why do you ask?"

Sliding his lips across her cheek, he nibbled at her lower lip. "I thought maybe you'd offer breakfast. I seem to be in need of sustenance."

Again, she captured his hand in the act of another illicit foray. "I haven't noticed that you're lacking for energy."

"All an act," he assured her mournfully. "I'm trying to keep up a macho front when in reality I'm weak with hunger." He kissed her deeply, thoroughly, leaving her trembling and gasping for breath. His own breathing was decidedly ragged when that kiss ended.

"You must be truly amazing when you're well fed," she whispered when she could speak.

"I'll give you the opportunity to find out," he promised with his most boyishly wicked smile. "After breakfast."

"All right. I can take a hint. I'll take a quick shower, then you can have the bathroom while I make breakfast."

He fell back on the pillows at the push of her hand. "Take your time," he offered generously. "But hurry."

She laughed, made a grab for her robe and headed for the bathroom.

Minutes later, Sabrina turned her face upward into the full spray of the shower, hoping to clear away the sleepiness still fogging her brain. Her knees quivered slightly, reminding her forcibly of the unaccustomed physical activity in which she had been a willing participant during the night. It was getting harder to convince herself that her feelings for Rob were nothing more than physical desire. And it was becoming increasingly important that she convince herself they could have nothing else.

She wanted Rob with a hunger that was new to her. So what was she going to do about it? And what results would their unplanned affair have on her orderly, regimented life? How would she feel when he was gone?

Reminding herself that Rob was no real threat to her carefully maintained routine, since she'd known all along that he was only passing through Dallas, she scooped her wet hair away from her face and reached for the shampoo. She told herself that it had been a wonderful weekend, that she should have no regrets about her behavior. What had it hurt to give in to her desires for a change, be irresponsible for the first time in longer than she could remember?

After all, she rationalized, she was a mature, modern woman and Rob an attractive, fascinating man. Why shouldn't she indulge her needs occasionally? Other women had affairs, took care of their sexual needs with little more consideration than they gave to their need for food and exercise and intellectual stimulation. Even Katherine, who was as fastidious as Sabrina, occasionally sought out male companionship. It wasn't as if Sabrina had intended to live the remainder of her life in celibacy, though she hadn't been particularly tempted to change that state until Rob had smiled at her in an elevator. She'd just never expected to find herself involved in a heated affair right now, particularly with a man she'd once known as "little Scooter Davis."

The shower curtain swept back, and the cool air against her wet skin made Sabrina shiver. She blinked water from her lashes just as Rob stepped into the tub to join her, his nude, glorious body glistening as the water cascaded over him. His lazy, sexy smile shattered her hazy memory of a small boy in grubby cutoffs. This was a man—all man—and he made Sabrina feel more a woman than anyone had before him.

Flushing at his intense regard, Sabrina tried to take cover behind a bar of soap. The little pink rectangle proved woefully inadequate for the task, as Rob's wandering, rapidly overheating gaze demonstrated. Lifting an eyebrow at the aroused condition of his magnificent body, she managed, "I thought you were hungry."

His laugh was nothing short of wicked. "I *was* hungry," he corrected, reaching for her. "Now I'm ravenous."

"I was going to make bacon and eggs," she murmured, her arms going automatically around his neck, bringing her wet body into full contact with his warm, supple skin.

"I've got a better idea." His voice was hoarse. Twisting to press her against the cool marble wall, he lifted her, draping her thighs around his hips.

Sabrina inhaled sharply when he lowered his head to lick the water from the tip of her left breast. Her voice strangled low in her throat, she agreed that his idea was much, much better than bacon and eggs. . . .

"Brie?"

"Mmm?" Without opening her eyes, she nuzzled more deeply into his shoulder, shifting to a more comfortable position on the damp sheets. There were certain disadvantages to falling into bed straight from the shower without taking time to dry off first. Of course, it had taken her quite a while to notice any discomfort.

"I'm starving."

She smiled against his collarbone. "Whose fault is that?"

"Yours."

"How do you figure that?"

"You refuse to feed me. You're holding me prisoner in this bedroom, ruthlessly distracting me every time I try to go in search of food."

"And just who was it who invaded whose shower? You could have been eating while I was in there, you know."

"That's exactly what I intended to do," he assured her mournfully. "Weak and disoriented with hunger, I stumbled to a door, hoping it was the door to the hallway. Instead, I fell right into your clutches again."

"I noticed your heroic efforts to escape."

He sighed. "Your will is too strong for me. I'm a helpless victim of your every demand."

She lifted her head, gave him her sweetest smile and summed up her response in one succinct, barnyard-oriented word.

"Not only is she merciless, she's potty-mouthed, too."

Sabrina blinked. "Potty-mouthed?" she repeated carefully.

He nodded, his blue eyes crinkled at the corners with the smile he refused to unleash. "A truly dangerous woman."

"And you, Rob Davis, are a very silly man," she informed him, lifting her nose an inch or so to add a lofty tone to the proclamation.

He laughed then, and hugged her tightly. "I knew you remembered how."

"Remembered how to what?" she asked breathlessly, her rib cage almost crushed by his exuberant embrace.

"How to play. It's kinda like riding a bike. Or having sex. Once you learn how . . ."

She placed a firm, silencing hand over his mouth, suddenly uncomfortable with the turn the conversation had taken. "Why don't we go eat now?"

He touched the tip of his tongue to her palm, sending tiny electric shocks from her wrist, up her arm and straight to her midsection. "Whatever you say, Brie," he murmured when she immediately jerked her hand away.

The man was incorrigible. And she knew that, despite her brave thoughts in the shower, she was going to miss him terribly when he was gone.

THEY'D JUST FINISHED a leisurely brunch and moved into the living room when the telephone rang. Sabrina lifted the receiver of the phone on the end table. "Hello."

"Hi, it's Katherine."

Sabrina suppressed a wince, expecting a third-degree about her dates with Rob. It wasn't that she didn't intend to talk about the weekend with Katherine; she'd just rather do it at a time when he wasn't listening. "Hi, Katherine."

"Listen, I'm really sorry to do this to you on a Sunday. I realize I'm taking advantage of our friendship for business purposes, but it's an emergency."

Obviously Katherine wasn't calling to grill her about Rob. "What's wrong?"

"I just got a call from the husband of one of the secretaries at the office. She was hospitalized this morning for emergency surgery. She couldn't help it, of course, but it's a terrible time for her to be away. We have a major board meeting first thing in the morning and I was already short-staffed, with two secretaries off on maternity leave at the same time."

"You need a temp in the morning," Sabrina translated, smiling at Katherine's uncharacteristically harried tone.

"Desperately," Katherine agreed. "Please tell me you can handle it."

"Have I ever let you down? I'll find someone."

"Oh, Sabrina, thanks. I owe you one."

Sabrina chuckled. "You'll get my bill."

"It will be worth it. By the way, about your date the other night . . ."

"Why don't we have lunch tomorrow and discuss it?" Sabrina suggested hastily, aware of Rob playing with Angel only a few feet away. "Or will you be tied up with the board meeting?"

"No, it should be over by noon. How about one o'clock at Salad Sally's?"

"Fine. I'll see you then. And I'll have a temp report to your office by eight, all right?"

"You're a godsend, Sabrina. Thanks again."

Sabrina hung up the phone and turned to Rob. "I have to go to my office and make some calls," she told him regretfully. "I have to find someone who can be ready to work first thing in the morning."

He smiled reassuringly. "I understand. I'd better be going anyway, I guess. My parents and I are supposed to have dinner tonight with my Aunt Mildred." He grimaced expressively as he said the name.

She laughed at his expression. "Not your favorite aunt?"

"Oh, she's okay. It's just that she's ninety years old and stone deaf, but she refuses to admit it. She'll spend all evening accusing me of muttering, even though I'll yell my throat raw trying to talk to her."

She knew full well that Rob would be untiringly patient with the elderly woman. She'd learned that much about him in the past few days—he was a genuinely nice man. "I'd better get dressed," she said, motioning toward the silk kimono she'd worn for their meal.

"Okay. I'll wait and leave when you do, if you don't mind." He seemed as reluctant as she to bring the weekend to an end.

She nodded. "Of course. Angel will be happy to entertain you while I get ready."

It took her only a few minutes to change into navy slacks and a red-and-white nautically-styled sweater. She ran a brush through her hair, then quickly put some makeup on. Checking her reflection, she noted her pensive expression and chided herself for it. She'd known the weekend had to end sometime, hadn't she? Lifting her chin determinedly, she left the room in search of Rob.

She'd just stepped out of her bedroom when she noticed that the door to the opposite room was open, the light on. Her throat tightened immediately. Was Rob . . . ?

She found him sitting at her desk, engrossed in the pages he'd found stacked beside the typewriter. Several pages lay beside him, already read, and as she watched, he turned over another, going on without pausing. He was reading her book! Reading what no one besides her had ever seen before, or even knew existed.

As if sensing her standing behind him, he looked up, his expression momentarily sheepish before he demanded, "Why didn't you tell me you're writing a novel?"

8

HER HANDS HAD STARTED to tremble. How silly. She clasped them behind her, forcing down the urge to snatch the pages away from him. "I'm not seriously writing a novel. It's just a hobby, something I do sometimes to relax after a particularly trying day at the office. I never intended for anyone to read it."

"Sabrina, this is good. Very good. The dialogue is natural and funny and the story line you've sketched out so far is enthralling. When it's finished, it—"

"When it's finished, if ever, I'll probably shove it in a drawer somewhere and start another one, for the same reason I play around with this one. Just to relax," she interrupted shortly, ignoring the unexpected thrill of pleasure from his praise. Did he really think she was good, or was he only saying so to be polite?

She pushed the question out of her mind, finally reaching out to take the stack of pages from him and replace them on the desk where he'd found them. "I told you, I don't have time to start another career and I'm perfectly content with the one I already have. It's taken me ages just to write this much. So, please, let's forget it."

"But, Brie—"

"Look, you really had no right to go through my things," she snapped, nerves suddenly frayed. "This was obviously something personal."

He stood, his expression shuttered. "You're right. I'm sorry."

She sighed, resisting the urge to apologize for her curtness. "I should go now. Are you ready?"

"Yeah, I guess so." He glanced back at the pages one last time as they left the room. Sabrina firmly snapped off the light and closed the door behind them.

Standing beside her car, which was parked in front of Rob's, she turned to him with a smile that felt false even to her. "It's been a very nice weekend, Rob. Thank you."

His brow shot up questioningly. "That sounds suspiciously like goodbye."

It was. She knew she had to bring this affair to an end now, while she still could. But, rather than argue with him about it—and she suspected that he *would* argue—she only smiled. "Well, goodbye for now, anyway," she amended lightly. "Tell Liz I said hello, will you? And your parents."

"Yes, I will. I'll call you tomorrow, all right?"

She unlocked her door, using that excuse to avoid looking at him. "Things may be pretty hectic at the office tomorrow. Mondays are always busy."

"So I'll call you at home." He spoke flatly, letting her know that she could expect the call.

Dammit, she thought wearily, why couldn't he see that there was really no reason for them to see each other again? He would be in town only another couple of weeks and then it would be over, anyway. If all he wanted was a diversion during that time, she was sure there were plenty of other women—young, spontaneous, fun-loving women who'd be more than happy to entertain him. Women who wouldn't be so foolish as to allow themselves to become too involved with him, dreading the time they'd have to say goodbye.

And there was always the other possibility that he was fulfilling a boyhood fantasy by going to bed with her. She really hated that one.

"'Bye, Rob," she said, opening her car door with every intention of climbing inside.

His hand on her arm whirled her around to face him. "Not so fast," he murmured.

She caught just a glimpse of his expression as he lowered his head to hers. Startled, she thought he looked angry. Why? But then he kissed her and she decided she must have been mistaken. His lips were gentle, his kiss almost lazily thorough. It lasted a very long time. When he finally released her, she found it necessary to clutch the car door for support, her knees having suddenly gone weak.

Rob smiled with what could have been interpreted as rather smug satisfaction. "See you, Brie."

And then he turned and sauntered toward his car, whistling cheerily beneath his teeth. Finding her gaze drawn to his very nice tush, Sabrina moaned softly and sank into her seat.

KATHERINE HARDLY GAVE Sabrina time to set her well-filled salad plate on the table Monday before leaning eagerly forward. "Well?"

Knowing exactly what her friend was asking, Sabrina stalled for time. "How did Carolyn work out in the secretarial opening this morning?"

Katherine answered impatiently. "She's working out beautifully, as you knew she would or you wouldn't have sent her. Tell me about your date."

"What date?"

"Sabrina," Katherine growled threateningly, hefting a butter knife in teasing menace.

Sabrina smiled and sliced into an oversized piece of lettuce. "Oh, all right, it was very nice."

Katherine waited for a long, meaningful moment. "Very nice?" she repeated finally. "That's all you're going to say?"

"What would you like for me to say?"

"Sabrina, Rob Davis is absolutely, stunningly, impossibly gorgeous. Not only that, he has sex-and-sin oozing out of every perfect pore. You're going to tell me a date with that man was nothing more than 'very nice'?"

Sex-and-sin. Good description, Sabrina mused, struck with an immediate mental photograph of Rob wearing nothing but a glint in his blue eyes and a deeply dimpled smile. Clearing her throat, she tried to keep her smile casual. "Okay, it was a gold medal date. On a scale of one to ten, this weekend was a fifty-nine. Does that make you happy?"

Katherine leaped on Sabrina's unconscious slip with avid interest. "The whole weekend?"

"Well—uh—we went out again Friday night. And we spent most of Saturday together."

Katherine eyed her speculatively. "You know, I had the distinct impression there was someone with you when I called yesterday morning. Was it by any chance—"

"Honestly, Katherine, you sound like a high school girl wanting to know how far I let him get."

Unperturbed, Katherine pressed on. "So how far *did* you let him get? First base? Or—" She paused for a dramatic change of voice, her eyes twinkling mischievously, "—home plate?"

Sabrina moaned and dropped her gaze to the food in front of her. "Do the words grand slam mean anything to you?"

Katherine clapped her hands in delight. "Details. I want details!"

Taking a deep breath, Sabrina started from the beginning. The Italian dinner Thursday, the lovely French restaurant Friday, the dancing, the unexpected flight to Galveston on Saturday. Katherine moaned in unconcealed envy, assuring Sabrina she'd never heard anything more romantic in her life.

"Lucky stiff. You did have an interesting weekend, didn't you?"

"You could say that."

"So . . . ?"

Sabrina winced. "So, it was wonderful, and I enjoyed every wicked minute of it, but it's over."

Frowning, Katherine swallowed a bite of salad before asking, "Why do you say that? Won't you be seeing him again?"

"I really don't see much point in it. He's leaving for Germany in a couple of weeks."

"Germany?"

"He's in the service. The air force. He's being stationed overseas for the next two years or so."

Katherine's shoulders sagged. "Damn."

Sabrina managed a weak smile. "Yeah. That about sums it up."

Her friend sighed deeply. "I had great hopes for this relationship. The two of you looked so right together. If ever I've seen a thoroughly smitten man, it was Rob in that pizza parlor."

Remembering her theory that Rob was only reliving a boyhood infatuation, Sabrina shrugged. "I think he enjoyed the challenge of talking me into going out with him. He seems to thrive on challenges."

"Did you ever find out how he knew so much about you?"

She groaned. "Yes."

"And?"

"I used to baby-sit him," Sabrina mumbled hurriedly.

"What?" Katherine had obviously not been able to understand her.

Taking a deep breath, Sabrina repeated the words more clearly. "I used to baby-sit him."

There was another long pause, during which Katherine slowly began to smile. "You used to *baby-sit* him?"

Her cheeks burning, Sabrina nodded. "Yes."

"Just how old *is* this guy?"

"Twenty-eight," Sabrina replied glumly.

Katherine moaned. "And you're letting him get away?"

"Uncle Sam is sending him away," Sabrina reminded her.

"So can't you set up a branch office in Germany or something? Hell, if you don't want him, *I* may follow him. Do you know how rare guys like that are?"

"Yes, I know." Sabrina never expected to find another man like Rob. The thought was too depressing to dwell on just then. Glancing at her watch, she noted the time with a sense of relief. "We'd better hurry. We both have to get back to our offices soon."

"You obviously want to change the subject."

Sabrina smiled apologetically. "If you don't mind. The weekend's still a bit too fresh in my mind for me to be totally objective."

"Could I ask just one more question?"

"What?" Sabrina asked warily.

Folding her hands in front of her, Katherine studied Sabrina's face with warm concern. "If things had been different, if Rob weren't shipping out soon, would he be the type of man you could fall for? Seriously, I mean."

Tempted to shrug off the disconcerting question, Sabrina made herself answer honestly, instead. After all, Katherine was her closest friend. "I don't know. I haven't allowed myself to think about it too much, since it's been clear from the start that there was no future in this. But—"

"But?" Katherine prodded gently.

Sabrina smiled sadly. "I don't think I'd have had very far to fall." She didn't add that she was half in love with him already. Some things were too private even to share with closest friends.

Katherine sighed. "Damn."

Sabrina looked at her watch again. "Guess I'd better get back to work."

"You're the boss at your place, remember? I'm the one who has to report to someone when I take too much time for lunch," Katherine complained, reaching for her purse. Again, there was just the faintest touch of envy in her throaty voice. She'd told Sabrina more than once that she'd love to someday own a business, having always dreamed of doing so.

Dreams again, Sabrina thought, handing some money to the obviously bored young woman behind the cash register. Always lurking at the back of one's mind, one's heart, just waiting to cause pain. It was a good thing she'd learned long ago not to invest too much in those ephemeral lures.

SABRINA STEPPED THROUGH the outer door to her offices, smiling politely at the rather nervous-looking, scantily dressed, too heavily accessorized young woman sitting stiffly in the waiting area. Must be her two-thirty appointment, she decided, studying the applicant surreptitiously as she stopped at Julia's desk for her messages. If the woman were at all qualified as a temporary, Sabrina would have to have a gentle talk with her about appropriate attire for work—and interviews. First, of course, she'd compliment her on her punctuality. She was ten minutes early.

"Ms. Chisum is here for her interview with you," Julia murmured, confirming Sabrina's guess at the woman's identity. And then she smiled mischievously and added,

"And there was a delivery while you were gone. I put it on your desk."

Rob, again. It had to be from the way Julia was smiling. "Thank you," Sabrina said, glancing at the six pink message slips she'd been given. Rob's name was on one of them. No number. "I'll be with you in just a moment, Ms. Chisum," she told the anxiously waiting applicant.

The woman smiled weakly and nodded.

Beverly was waiting at Sabrina's door. Beverly, Sabrina thought, knew exactly how to dress to appear both professional and undeniably feminine. The lacy cream blouse she wore with a tan linen suit perfectly complemented the young woman's flawless dark complexion. Sabrina applauded herself again for having excellent taste in hiring, a handy talent in her line of work. "I need your signature, Sabrina," Beverly announced, holding out an official-looking form and a pen.

Sabrina carried the form to her desk and signed her name neatly at the bottom. Only then did she allow herself to look at the sumptuous bouquet of yellow roses sitting on one corner of her desk. Their beauty made her go all soft inside, despite her efforts to be strong. There was no card, but then a card hadn't been necessary. She knew who'd sent them. "Damn the man," she muttered, unable to resist reaching out to stroke one velvety half-opened bloom.

"He'd have had me with the balloons," Beverly commented in amusement. "But who could possibly resist a dozen yellow roses?"

"Tell Julia to send Ms. Chisum in, will you, Beverly? She should be ready for testing in a half hour or so."

Taking the hint that Sabrina didn't want to talk about the roses or Rob, Beverly nodded. "All right. Buzz me when she's ready."

Sabrina took advantage of the next three minutes alone to remind herself sternly that she was not going to fall for Rob Davis, no matter how many sweet gestures he made. The man was good, she'd give him that. But she swore he'd have no broken heart to leave behind in this particular port.

ROB CALLED TWICE during the afternoon. Both times Sabrina cravenly asked Julia to take a message, claiming to be much too busy to talk to him. The messages said only that he'd call again later.

The monthly dinner meeting of an organization for women business owners was scheduled for that evening. Sabrina lingered at the office until time to leave for the meeting, knowing full well she was avoiding Rob. She told herself she was only being sensible in ending a relationship that had nowhere to go but heartache, though a tiny, scornful voice in the back of her mind argued that she was merely being a coward. Better a coward than an utter fool, she mentally retorted, effectively silencing that voice.

It was nearly ten when she entered her front door that evening, grateful for Angel's enthusiastic greeting. Spotting the blinking light on her answering machine, she grimaced, took a deep breath and pressed the play button.

Rob's deep voice went through her like warm molasses, causing her to sink bonelessly into a chair. "Hi, it's Rob. You've been really busy today, haven't you? I'll try again tomorrow. Sweet dreams, Brie."

There'd been no hint of accusation in his words, but she still sensed that he knew she'd deliberately avoided him. Just as she understood that he wouldn't stop calling until she talked to him again. Why, Rob? she moaned silently, one hand over her eyes. What are you trying to prove?

Sweet dreams. Did he know she'd dream of him?

Her steps heavy, she climbed the stairs to her bedroom, where she made a deliberate effort not to look at the big, empty bed as she changed into comfortable pink pajamas made of soft cotton knit. She knew she wouldn't be able to go to sleep just then, so she drifted into the bedroom across the hall. For a long time she simply sat at the desk, staring at the stack of pages in front of her.

Rob had said her writing was good. Had he meant it? Had he only been polite? Had he read enough in that scant half hour to judge objectively?

A long time ago she'd been told she had talent as a writer. Teachers in high school, in college, had praised her work and encouraged her to pursue it. She'd intended to do so then. She'd thought there was plenty of time after she'd established the family she'd craved more than publication. But then that dream had fallen through and she'd tried to ignore the other as she'd set to work building a successful business.

She'd told Rob she didn't have time to begin a second career. But still she found herself in front of this typewriter, again and again, the stack of finished pages slowly growing. Why? Was it truly no more than a hobby, a stress-reliever? Or was that old dream still alive, the embers still glowing beneath the ashes of other disappointments?

He'd said it was good. Picking up the last page she'd written, Sabrina read it carefully. Maybe he was right. Maybe it *was* good. Pulling her lower lip between her teeth, she rolled a fresh sheet of paper into the typewriter. She'd decide what to do with the book after she finished it, she told herself. For now, she had a story to tell. Setting her hands to the keys, she began to type, the words flowing onto the page even as the tension slowly began to ease from her weary shoulders.

"ANOTHER DELIVERY, Sabrina." Julia's voice was almost gleeful as she carried a neatly wrapped package into Sabrina's office on Wednesday afternoon.

Sabrina wasn't even surprised. Rob had called twice the day before, but she'd managed to be busy each time. He hadn't called today, but she'd half expected another of his attempts to charm her into . . . whatever it was he wanted from her. She still hadn't quite decided what that was.

Julia hovered by the desk after handing Sabrina the package. "Aren't you going to open it?" she asked in dismay when Sabrina only set it aside.

Sabrina sighed. "It's going to drive you crazy until I do, isn't it?"

"Of course!"

Reaching for the package, Sabrina sighed again. "All right, if it will make you happy."

Julia tapped one foot meaningfully. "Don't try to convince me you're not even curious. You're only using me for an excuse to open it."

Sabrina prudently decided not to comment. After all, Julia was right. She *was* curious about what Rob had sent this time.

The expensive filled chocolates were shaped like seashells. Looking at them, Sabrina's thoughts were immediately swept back to that romantic evening in Galveston. Just as he'd planned, of course. "Damn."

Julia whistled softly between her teeth. "If you can hold out much longer against this guy, you have to be made of steel. He's good."

Oh, yes, he was good. At much more than skillful pursuit. Sabrina surrendered to the inevitable. Evading his call again would be unconscionably rude. "If he calls again, put him through, all right?"

Julia grinned. "You bet."

She didn't have to wait long. Rob called less than an hour later. "I was beginning to think you were a figment of my imagination," he accused her.

"I'm sorry. I've been busy," she offered lamely. "Thank you for the flowers and the chocolates, Rob. But you really should stop sending gifts."

"Have dinner with me tonight?" he asked, ignoring the gentle remonstration.

"I'm sorry, I can't. I have plans."

"Another date?"

Though he'd obviously tried to ask lightly, his tone was suspiciously sharp. Sabrina got the impression that he wouldn't be at all pleased if she said yes. Why? she asked herself in exasperation at his motives. What could it possibly matter to him if she had another date? "Actually, I'm baby-sitting tonight," she admitted. "My neighbors have a ten-year-old daughter with cerebral palsy. I have her over to watch movies with me occasionally so her parents can go out to dinner. They need a break at times."

"That's very nice of you."

"I enjoy Mandy's company."

"So will you need any help baby-sitting? I make a mean bowl of popcorn."

"Thanks for the offer, but we were planning an all-girl evening. You know, experimenting with makeup, doing our nails, giggling about boys."

Rob accepted the excuse without argument. "How about having lunch with me tomorrow, instead?"

She could handle lunch, she decided. That was safe enough. Maybe over lunch she'd be able to tactfully let Rob know she was hesitant to continue their affair during his remaining time in Dallas. But how could she tell him without revealing her worst fear—that she was in danger of losing her heart to him?

"What's wrong, Brie?" Rob asked when she'd hesitated just a bit too long. "Running out of excuses?"

"Lunch tomorrow will be fine, Rob," she answered coolly.

"Good. I'll pick you up at noon."

"All right. I'll see you then."

"Have fun with your little friend tonight."

"I'm sure I will. I really must get back to work now. Goodbye, Rob."

"See you tomorrow, Brie."

She hung up the phone and buried her face in her hands.

ROB PUT DOWN THE PHONE in his sister's den with a scowl. He took some pride in knowing that he'd adequately concealed his growing irritation with Sabrina. It had become perfectly clear that she'd been avoiding him, finding excuses not to talk to him or see him. He thought she'd probably only agreed to lunch because she'd known he wouldn't stop asking until she accepted.

He wouldn't have been put off much longer before he'd have stormed her home or office and forced her to see him. He wanted to see her again, dammit. Hell, he couldn't seem to think of anything else.

He'd reacted to Sabrina in a way that had rather amazed him. It had been a while since he'd been involved with a woman. Rob had never been one to take sex casually, despite his enjoy-the-minute attitude about everything else. But that lengthy period of abstinence had nothing to do with his incredible response to Sabrina Marsh. Rather, it was Sabrina herself. Beautiful, bright, capable, cautious, passionate Sabrina.

Passionate. The word repeated itself in his mind, making him smile reflectively. She was that. He suspected that the depths of her passion had even startled her, judging from the expressions he'd surprised on her face a time or two. Or was that only wishful thinking on his part? Was he only hoping her reactions to him had been unprecedented because he'd never experienced anything like what they'd shared with any of the select few women before her? He felt as if he'd been waiting his whole life for her, saving some special, secret part of himself to reveal only to her. And he had. Over and over.

And now she was avoiding him. Telling herself he was only a safe, reasonably attractive man just passing through town. She'd indulged her needs with him, then tried to escape back into her safe, cautious, regimented life.

She had a lot to learn about this particular man. When Rob Davis found something he wanted, he tended to go after it, regardless of the odds against him. And he wanted Sabrina. Badly. Even if for only the remaining two weeks he'd have with her before he had to leave. He tried not to think of the time when they'd have to part. Unlike Sabrina, he wouldn't allow that inevitable moment to dim his pleasure in what they could have now.

Yes, he thought with a grim smile, Sabrina had a lot to learn about him.

IT WAS A LONG DAY at the office. Sabrina arrived home tired and dispirited, her convoluted feelings about Rob only adding to her general weariness. She wasn't particularly hungry, but she ate a sandwich and drank a glass of milk. She thought about working on her book for a while, but for once the lure of the story couldn't distract her from her problems. Instead, she sat down to watch the ten o'clock news with Angel, deciding it was time to catch up on world events.

The closing feature story was a report of a navy carrier pulling out for a six-month sea tour. There were plenty of those poignant shots the public seemed to love so much. An elderly woman kissing her son goodbye. Small children crying as they hugged their uniformed daddies. A very pregnant woman smiling bravely as she saw her husband off, knowing she'd soon go through childbirth alone.

Sabrina turned off the set with a vicious snap. She knew Rob would have to leave soon, too. Worse, he'd be at the forefront of military intervention, should a war break out anywhere in the world.

Dammit, Rob, why'd you have to be in the service? she thought almost angrily, pacing the length of the living room with a vehemence that seemed to surprise her dog. *Why couldn't you have been an airline pilot, or owned your own charter service? Why'd you have to be in that particular elevator on that particular day? And why won't you let me go before I do something really stupid—like fall in love with you?*

9

"A BABY STORE?" Sabrina asked curiously, glancing at Rob as he parked his car in front of Baby World after picking her up for lunch on Thursday. "You take me to the most surprising places, Rob."

He grinned and pulled off his sunglasses, dropping them in the console between them. "Liz ordered something here that came in this morning. I told her I'd pick it up for her. It'll just take a minute. Want to come in with me?"

Sabrina shrugged. "Sure." She reached for her door handle.

While Rob took care of his sister's purchase, Sabrina wandered idly around the store, looking over the nursery furnishings, tiny accessories, new baby care items she'd never even heard of. Admiring a tiny ruffled dress, she remembered a time when she'd dreamed of holding her own baby. A rather painful memory of a heated conversation with her ex-husband—one in which he'd made it quite clear he wasn't ready for the responsibilities of fatherhood—made her wince and turn away from the rack of frilly garments.

She was thirty-three years old. Chances were she'd never have a child of her own now. She'd told herself that she'd come to grips with that possibility. After all, she firmly believed a child needed two parents and she had no intention of marrying just so she'd have a father for a baby. Yet she still found herself facing those old maternal longings she'd thought long since conquered. She'd have been a good mother, she decided with a wistful sigh.

"Look at this, Brie. Cute, huh?"

Obediently, she turned to Rob, who stood behind her admiring a teddy bear dressed in a Dallas Cowboys football uniform. "It's adorable," she assured him.

He grinned and lifted the stuffed toy from the shelf. "I think I'll buy it for my nephew."

"How do you know it's a boy?"

Shrugging, he shoved the bear under his arm and wandered to another display case. "Just a guess. What do you suppose these things are?"

Sabrina moved to stand beside him. "Haven't you seen those before? They're used to keep track of active toddlers. The mother straps this end around her wrist and this other end around the child's and this stretch cord between lets the kid walk around without getting too far."

"That's a good idea," Rob decided. "I'll get one for Liz."

"Rob, the baby won't even walk for a year or so."

"So she'll be prepared." He picked out a package and handed it to her. "Hold this for me, will you? Hey, look at that!"

Indulgently, Sabrina followed him from one display to another, laughing as he found "one more thing" his sister really needed. "You're not excited about this baby, are you, Rob?" she accused him teasingly, charmed by his enthusiasm.

He grinned sheepishly. "Yeah. I am. Damn, I wish she'd hurry and have it. I'd really like to see the baby before I leave."

Sabrina's smile dimmed. She turned her head so Rob wouldn't notice. "Look at the little shoes. Can you imagine a foot that tiny?"

"I like the ones with the little ruffles and rosebuds," Rob remarked, glancing over her shoulder.

Her emotions firmly under control, Sabrina chuckled. "Your nephew would look kind of silly in those, wouldn't he?"

His dimples flashed. "Well, it could be a girl. Just in case, I think I'll get them. Liz can always trade them in for the little wing-tips if necessary."

By the time they left the store, Rob had quite a stack of purchases, including the nursery lamp Liz had specially ordered to match her decor. Sabrina helped him carry the load to his car and stash it in the back seat. "Your nephew—or niece—is very lucky to have such a generous uncle," she commented, climbing into her own seat and reaching for the seat belt.

"You should see what my parents have already bought for this child," Rob told her cheerfully, starting the car. "The kid's going to be spoiled rotten, being the first grandchild."

"D'you think Liz and Gordon will have other children?"

He shrugged. "I'm sure they will, if they can. Liz loves kids."

Sabrina gave him a sideways smile. "Something tells me she's not the only one."

"No," he admitted. "I'd like to have a couple of my own someday. Wouldn't you?"

Murmuring something noncommittal, Sabrina quickly changed the subject. Rob allowed her to do so, though she was aware that he gave her a searching look across the console before following her conversational lead.

He waited until they had almost finished their lunch before dropping the light, casual tone they'd affected until then. Leaning his forearms on the table in the secluded corner of the restaurant he'd selected, he looked steadily at her as he asked, "Why have you been avoiding me this week, Brie?"

Caught by surprise, she nearly choked on her broiled fish. She reached quickly for her water glass, took a sip and then lowered it. "What makes you think I've been avoiding you, Rob?" she asked. "I told you I've been very busy this week."

"Yes, that's what you've told me," he agreed, his eyes steady. "But that's not the real reason you've been so reluctant to see me, is it?"

She started to prevaricate, to tell him she hadn't the faintest idea what he was talking about. One glance at his face changed her mind. Rob knew exactly what she'd been doing and the reason why. So why was he forcing the issue now? "All right," she said at length, unable to keep a certain defensiveness from her voice, "I suppose I have been looking for excuses."

"Why?"

Pushing her plate away, she spread her hands in a gesture of discomfiture. "Because I don't see any point in going on with this," she admitted. "You're leaving soon and you should want to spend time with your family before you go. You and I barely know each other, after all."

"Brie," he murmured chidingly. "That's hardly true."

She flushed and glanced away. "I didn't mean physically. I only meant that there's no future to our continuing to see each other. You're on your way overseas, I'm quite firmly rooted here. I'm not really the type to indulge in temporary affairs. It—"

He interrupted her with a quiet question. "Are you feeling guilty that we've made love?"

"Of course not," she denied immediately. "We haven't done anything wrong. We're both mature adults and what we had was wonderful. But—"

Her words faded into silence when he reached across the table, caught her hand and lifted it to his lips. "I like being with you, Sabrina. We have a good time together, we enjoy many of the same things. We have fun. Is that so bad?"

"No, Rob," she whispered tightly. "It's not bad. But—"

"There's no way I can stay in Dallas for the next two weeks without wanting to see you again. It's silly for us to try to avoid each other during that time since it's so nice when we're together. Don't you agree?"

"Well, I—"

"Do you really want to say goodbye now?"

She stared at him, her hand limp in his warm grasp. Of course she didn't want to say goodbye now, she thought sadly. The problem was that she was beginning to think she'd never want to say goodbye to him. Would it really be easier to end this now, or should she take advantage of this opportunity to have two more weeks with him? Two more weeks of romantic dinners, dancing, laughter? Two more weeks of the kind of passion she was sure most women only fantasized about?

"I'm no threat to you, Brie," he murmured as if he knew what she was thinking. "I only want to make you happy."

She almost laughed at that, though the sound would have held little amusement. No threat? He had no idea. He'd already disrupted the comfortable, secure routines she'd fallen into over the past few years. Would her life ever be the same when he left it? But common sense proved to be no competition to the seductive entreaty of his bright blue eyes, his slow, sexy smile. Damn the man, she thought for at least the hundredth time. Had any woman ever been able to resist him? She sighed lightly and pulled her hand away from his.

Though she still hadn't spoken, Rob must have read the capitulation in her expression. His smile deepened. "Will you go to a movie with me tonight?"

"Yes."

"Thank you."

She nodded and reached for her purse, refusing his offer of dessert with the valid excuse that she needed to get back to the office.

You really are a fool, Sabrina Marsh, she told herself in annoyed exasperation.

SABRINA HATED FIRING people. It always left her in a grumpy mood. Which was exactly the way she felt Friday afternoon after dismissing a temp who'd gathered complaints at her last three assignments. The woman had a real problem handling responsibilities, which was the reason she hadn't been able to hold on to any full-time job for very long. Seeing potential behind the carelessness, Sabrina had hoped to guide the young woman into more reliable behavior. She didn't like to admit defeat, but neither could she afford to have a less-than-satisfactory employee affiliated with her business.

Glancing at the clock on her office wall, she noted in relief that it was after five. Julia had already left for the weekend, Beverly wouldn't be far behind. Soon Sabrina could escape, as well. Her mood lightened considerably when she thought of the time she'd spend later with Rob.

Rob. Just the thought of him could make her smile, and then sigh. He'd chosen a fluffy romantic comedy movie the evening before, not one Sabrina would have selected at all. She'd loved it. They'd laughed until tears had rolled, holding hands and sharing popcorn like two carefree teenagers. There hadn't been nearly enough laughter in her life during the past few years. She hadn't even been aware of the lack until Rob had come along and shown her how much fun she could have with him.

He hadn't spent the night, but had left her at her door, saying he knew she had to get up early the next morning for work. He'd kissed her half-senseless before he left, tempting her strongly to forget about the next morning and drag him off to bed. But she'd let him go. She'd spent a good half hour afterward wondering if Rob hadn't pressed to stay because he'd sensed how confused she felt about their relationship. Maybe he was a bit confused himself.

Beverly poked her head around Sabrina's half-opened office door. "I'm out of here, boss. Unless you need anything else before I go?"

Sabrina shook her head. "I'm on my way out, myself. See you Monday."

"Got a date tonight?" Beverly waited with barely concealed avidness for Sabrina's answer.

"Yes, Beverly, I have a date tonight."

"With Rob?"

"With Rob."

Beverly grinned broadly. "Way to go, girl."

Sabrina only grimaced and waved good-night.

Parking her car in her driveway less than an hour later, Sabrina reached for her purse, thinking about what she'd wear for the date, already speculating about how this evening might end. This time there was no work waiting the next morning as an excuse, no reason at all Rob shouldn't spend the night. No reason except that it would be one more night for the bond between them to grow even stronger. Maybe she'd better play it by ear, she decided, unwilling to make the decision just yet.

Hailed from her neighbor's porch, she looked up to find Mandy and her father enjoying the last rays of the afternoon sun. "Hi, Mandy. Hello, Terry."

Terry O'Neal nodded, his thinning hair ruffled around his habitually serious face by the gentle breeze that caught at

Mandy's fluffy bangs and rippled the skirt of Sabrina's blue knit dress. "Hi, Sabrina. How was your day?"

"The usual. Things going okay at the university?" she asked politely, falling into their usual pattern of neighborly small talk.

"Yes, just fine."

"I got a new dress, Sabrina. It's red."

"Good for you, Mandy. I'd love to see you in it."

"I get to wear it to church Sunday."

"I'm sure you'll look beautiful in it."

Mandy grinned broadly, pigtailed head bobbing, then frowned with interest as a black sports car pulled into Sabrina's driveway. "Who's that?"

"That's my date," Sabrina replied as Rob climbed out of his car. "He's a bit early."

"I guess he couldn't wait to see you," Mandy quipped. She studied Rob appraisingly as he approached. "Wow! What a hunk!" she exclaimed, her squeaky young voice carrying clearly.

"Very definitely a hunk," Sabrina agreed, making Rob grin. "Rob Davis," she went on as he came to a stop beside her. "I'd like you to meet my friends. This is Terry O'Neal and his daughter, Mandy."

Rob shook Terry's hand then smiled down at Mandy, his eyes softening as he quickly took in the wheelchair and the child's awkward movements within it. "Hi, Mandy. It's very nice to meet you."

Mandy solemnly extended an unsteady hand, saying in her most grown-up voice, "How do you do, Mr. Davis. It's nice to meet you, too."

"Mandy was just telling me about her new red dress," Sabrina explained, smiling at the girl. "I think it may be a reward for getting one hundred percent on a big math test last week."

"One hundred percent? Gosh, I'm impressed," Rob said immediately. "I didn't get many of those in school."

Mandy giggled in delight.

Knowing how Mandy loved watching the planes take off and land at the Dallas-Fort Worth airport on outings with her parents, Sabrina told her that Rob was a pilot.

Mandy's eyes widened. "Really? You're really a pilot?"

"I really am. I'm in the air force," Rob assured her.

"Why aren't you wearing your uniform?"

"I'm on leave. I don't usually wear it when I'm off duty."

"I'd sure like to see you in it," Mandy told him wistfully.

Sabrina realized that she wouldn't mind seeing Rob in uniform, herself. She'd bet he looked spectacular in it. But then, Rob looked that way all the time.

"I like you, Rob," Mandy told him ingenuously. "Sabrina said you were early and I said you prob'ly couldn't wait to see her. Was I right?"

Rob laughed. "You were exactly right. I've been looking forward to seeing Sabrina all day."

"She's nice, isn't she?"

"Very."

"I'd better get inside. Angel's having fits in there," Sabrina put in hastily, before Mandy's matchmaking got even more embarrassing. "See you later, Mandy."

Rob chuckled as he followed Sabrina into her living room. "She's something else, isn't she?" he asked, fending off Angel's fervent greeting.

"Mandy's a dear," Sabrina agreed.

"You're very good with her."

She tossed her purse onto the secretary and smoothed her slightly crumpled skirt. "So were you."

"Do you like all children, Brie, or just Mandy?" He crossed his arms casually in front of him, watching her face as he waited for her answer.

"I love children, though I'm not around them very often," she admitted.

"You never really answered me yesterday when I asked if you ever want children of your own. Do you?"

She cleared her throat and made a production of glancing through her mail when she answered lightly, "There was a time when I wanted children. Now, well, I've faced the fact that I'm not getting any younger."

"You're only thirty-three. You have plenty of time for children."

"Yes, well, who knows." Shying away from the serious subject, she dropped the mail beside her purse and glanced toward the kitchen. "Would you like something to drink while I change?"

"Are children another dream you've put away, Sabrina?" Rob asked quietly, moving to stand very close to her. "Like your writing?"

She shifted uncomfortably. "Rob—"

He sighed. "Never mind. I can tell you aren't going to answer that one. How about a kiss, instead? I've been craving a Sabrina Marsh kiss all day."

Deeply relieved at the change of subject, she lifted her face. "All you had to do was say so."

He smiled and covered her lips with his. Sabrina sighed imperceptibly into his mouth, thinking that maybe she wouldn't send him away that evening, after all. Already her body was quivering into heated anticipation of making love with him again.

IT TURNED OUT THAT Rob didn't give her a choice. He took her to dinner, then for drinks and dancing. They had a wonderful time. She reveled in being in his arms on the dance floor, in the intimate conversation they shared, in the wanton expectations of what would follow. She practically reeled in frustrated shock when he kissed her good-night at her door, obviously intending to walk away afterward.

"You really don't have to go, Rob. It's still early," she murmured, clinging to his lapel when he would have stepped away.

Though he was clearly tempted, he smiled tenderly and gently removed her hand. "My parents are expecting me tonight," he told her. "I'd better go. Will you spend tomorrow with me?"

"Yes," she answered, trying to hide the extent of her disappointment.

He smiled. "I'll pick you up in the morning, around ten. Dress casually."

"All right. Good night, Rob."

He kissed her again, quickly, his hands held safely at his sides. "G'night, Brie. Sweet dreams."

She stepped inside her living room, closed and locked the door, then rested her head against the wood surface with a groan that brought Angel inquiringly to her side. Why hadn't Rob wanted to stay? Didn't he still want her? She remembered being held close to him on the dance floor, the very obvious evidence that he had wanted her then. No, the attraction between them was still very strong. So why was he resisting? Was he only being considerate to her concerns about a fleeting affair, reacting to her admission that she was uncertain about continuing it?

Don't do me any more favors, Rob, she thought with a sigh, glancing toward the stairs as she debated the benefits of a cold shower. She didn't expect to get much sleep that night. Maybe she'd work some more on her book.

SABRINA WAS FULLY DRESSED a half hour before Rob was due to pick her up the next morning. Studying herself in the mirror, she frowned, wondering if her choice of gray linen slacks and a pink-and-gray striped cotton sweater were appropriate for whatever activities he had in mind for the day. She'd pulled her hair into a loose French braid to keep it out of the way. She wondered if a jaunty pink bow at the base would make the style look more youthful. And then her frown turned to a scowl as she realized exactly what she was doing. A perky bow could not change the fact that she was five years older than Rob, nor erase his memories—or her own—of the time they'd known each other before.

Angel announced Rob's arrival even before the doorbell rang as he raced to the door, barking a welcome. Sabrina was smiling when she opened the door. "Good morning."

He leaned over to kiss her lightly, then drew back. "You look very nice."

"Thank you." She eyed his short sleeved black pullover and jeans. The jeans were so old that both knees were ripped seam to seam, pockets and fly frayed and faded to near white. He looked sexy enough to attack on the spot. And she was beginning to feel overdressed.

Rob's smile told her he'd read her mind again. "You'll probably want to change," he murmured gently, passing her into the living room. "Do you *own* a pair of jeans?"

"Of course I have jeans," she retorted rather indignantly. "You just didn't tell me we were going quite this casual."

"Sorry." His expression was bland. "My mistake."

She looked suspiciously at him, but he only smiled back at her. Finally she sighed and nodded. "I'll change. Would you like a cup of coffee?"

"I'd love it. Thanks." He followed her into the kitchen, one hand on Angel's neck as the dog trailed happily at his side.

She set his coffee cup on the table. "The morning paper's here if you'd like to read it. It won't take me long to change."

Walking up the stairs to her room, she found her thoughts filled with Rob, with her strong feelings for him. They had really only known each other for just under two weeks, yet time seemed to hold little meaning for them. The sense of knowing him so well had little to do with that year in Irving. Her heart had been captured by Rob, the man, not Rob, the child-memory.

Her heart? Oh, damn, had it finally come to that?

She sat on the edge of her bed and dropped her face into her hands, trying to remind herself once again that Rob would soon be gone.

Several moments later, she drew a deep, bracing breath and stood, opening her closet door to pull a pair of jeans from a shelf. This pair was much newer and more fashionable than the ones Rob had on, but her selection was rather limited. She really didn't own many jeans. Pairing them with a bright yellow cotton sweater, she chewed her lower lip as she laced nearly new running shoes over a pair of yellow socks, still thinking of Rob.

Exactly what was going on inside that attractive head of his? She simply couldn't believe that he was only playing games with her. For some reason, she suspected that his feelings for her were more than fleeting. He'd made love to her with more than his body, making himself vulnerable to her even as she lost herself in him. And what was that rather clumsy questioning about children? She could understand that he was at an age when men started thinking about marriage and children, but surely he wasn't starting to think of those things in reference to her! She was too firmly settled in Dallas, a woman five years older than himself, whose childbearing years were becoming limited by her biological clock. She couldn't be more for him than the vacation affair she'd become.

Her thoughts kept coming around to the possibility that he was living a boyhood fantasy. Sabrina understood infatuation. She had been so hopelessly smitten with Burt that she'd married him mostly out of gratitude that he'd even asked her.

Sabrina's first love had ended abruptly and disillusioningly. Now Rob had found his first crush. Unfortunately, she was now an adult, with an adult's experiences behind her, having learned to put away dreams and childhood fantasies. He'd get over his infatuation when he fully realized that she was no longer a fifteen-year-old "dream girl" but a thirty-three-year-old woman with a few lines just starting around her eyes and a lot of emotional baggage from the past.

But would she ever get over him?

"Sabrina?" Rob's voice startled her; she hadn't realized he'd entered the room. She blinked, finding him kneeling beside the tiny dresser chair in which she sat, his face grave with concern. "Sweetheart, is something wrong?"

Sabrina forced a smile. "No, of course nothing's wrong. Why do you ask?"

"You looked sad when I came in. So far away." He lifted her hand to his lips. "Tell me what's bothering you."

"I was just thinking," she answered evasively, resisting an impulse to throw herself into his arms and hold on to him.

"About us?" he asked with that uncanny perception he displayed all too often.

"Yes," she answered honestly.

"Talk to me."

She shook her head. "No. Not now. Please."

He looked as though he wanted to argue, but something in her face must have warned him to let it drop. He sighed, stood and pulled her into his arms. "We have so much to talk about. Soon. But today we'll just enjoy being together. Deal?"

"Deal." She kissed him to seal the agreement, then stepped out of his arms. Standing in front of her mirrored dresser, she checked to make sure her French braid hadn't been disarrayed by her changing clothes.

Rob dropped to the edge of the bed and leaned back on his hands as he watched her dab a touch of lip gloss on her mouth. "Lady, I like the way those jeans fit," he murmured. "Very nice."

"Thank you." Something in his expression told her he was tired of gallantly keeping his distance, giving her time.

"Come here."

She tilted her head suspiciously, hands on her hips as she eyed the mischief on his face. "Why?"

His eyebrows shot up devilishly.

"But I just got dressed—again," she protested, smiling despite herself. Her pulse began a heavy quickening in response to the banked hunger in his eyes.

"Come here and let me make sure you didn't forget anything," he challenged with answering humor, holding out his hand.

She had taken two steps toward him when the telephone rang.

Rob groaned. "Whoever that is has lousy timing."

Sabrina chuckled and lifted the receiver. "Hello?"

"Guess what I brought you from Africa."

"Oh, no, not an elephant. I can barely keep Angel fed." She plopped down on the bed beside Rob, clutching the receiver with pleasure. "When did you get back, Colin? I wasn't expecting you until next week."

"Finished early. Got home an hour ago."

"You're talking like a telegram," Sabrina mocked her brother affectionately, delighted to hear his voice for the first time in six weeks. "How are you?"

"Sunburned and mosquito bitten, but several thousand dollars richer. The shoot went beautifully. The publisher was delighted."

"Well, good for you." She glanced at Rob, who was making motions to leave her in privacy. "You don't have to leave, Rob," she told him quickly, forgetting to cover the phone. "It's Colin, my brother."

Rob hesitated.

Colin asked interestedly, "Who the hell is Rob? That's a new one."

"Rob's a—uh—a friend," she stammered, making Rob frown. Well, what did he expect her to say, she wondered in mild exasperation. The situation was a bit complicated, to say the least.

"Oh? Do I know him?"

"In a way," she answered. Rob made a restless motion with his hand, indicating he'd wait for her downstairs, and left the room, leaving Sabrina staring after him in bewilderment. What had suddenly changed his mood?

"Brie? You still there?"

Remembering her brother, she cleared her throat. "Sure."

"So who's this Rob?" he persisted like the curious younger sibling he was.

"Rob Davis. Remember the Davises who lived down the street from us in Irving?"

Colin thought for a moment. "Yeah, vaguely. They had a couple of little kids and lots of cousins who used to come over for picnics and ball games and stuff. Right?"

"Right."

"I don't remember one called Rob."

Sabrina's mouth twisted. "Remember the one they called Scooter?"

"Scooter? Sure, I remember him. Skinny little kid." Colin's voice suddenly grew sharper. "They call him Rob now, by any chance?"

"Yes, as a matter of fact, they do."

"You mean you've got Scooter Davis in your bedroom?"

"How did you know I'm in my bedroom?" Sabrina countered defensively.

"I do now. Imagine you and little Scooter Davis."

"You can be so obnoxious, Colin. Rob's hardly a child now. He's a grown man, only three years younger than you are. We ran into each other by accident on Tuesday and we've been spending some time together since."

"Of course I haven't seen him in nearly twenty years, but it's hard to imagine the two of you ... spending time together." Colin put a meaningful emphasis on the last three words.

"Please don't tease me about this," Sabrina asked quietly, hearing her own vulnerability in her voice.

Her brother paused, knowing her well enough to understand the nuances of her tone. "Sorry, Brie. I didn't mean to offend you."

"You didn't." She quickly changed the subject. "I'm glad you're home. How's Casey? Have you talked to her yet?"

"No, not yet. I'll call her in a minute."

"You mean you called your sister before your girlfriend? I'm flattered."

"You should be. Strangely enough, I missed you, Sis. Tell Sc—uh, Rob, I said hello."

"I will. Tell Casey the same from me." Sabrina hung up the telephone and looked toward the doorway through which Rob had disappeared. And then she stood, squared her shoulders and went off in search of him.

10

SHE FOUND HIM SITTING on the couch in the living room, an old Western movie playing on the TV, Angel curled sleepily at his feet. Rob looked up when she came in. "So, how's your brother?"

"He's fine." And then she couldn't help asking, "It bothered you that Colin called. Why?"

He stood, ran a hand through his short dark hair, then pushed both hands into the pockets of his snug-fitting jeans. "It didn't—"

"I thought you said you'd never lie to me," she broke in firmly.

His mouth twisted. "Yeah. Okay, it bothered me."

"Why?"

He lifted one shoulder in a sheepish shrug. "Because I knew what his reaction would be when you told him who I am. He laughed, didn't he?"

"Well, he—uh—"

Looking glum, he nodded. "I thought so. He thinks I'm too young for you, doesn't he?"

"What Colin thinks doesn't really matter," Sabrina replied firmly. "This—affair is just between us."

Rob smiled and reached for her. Taking her by surprise, he kissed her until her ears buzzed and she clung to him like wet spaghetti, then released her so abruptly she nearly collapsed at his feet. Grinning, he steadied her. "You'd better get a jacket."

She took several deep breaths, trying to bring her pulse under control. "Why do I need a jacket? It's supposed to get up to seventy degrees today."

"You won't need it once we get there, but the trip may be a bit windy. Get with it, woman, we've got things to do."

"Like what? Where are we going? And why will the trip be windy?"

"Trust me, okay?"

She stared at him. Trust him? Sure. With a stifled sigh, she turned to get her jacket.

Rob was watching Sabrina's face when she stepped out her front door a few minutes later. She stopped in her tracks to stare at the vehicle in the driveway. "You don't really expect me to get on that, do you?"

He laughed. "I certainly do."

She looked from him to the large motorcycle parked behind her car, and then back again. "Uh-uh. No way. We'll take my car."

"Oh, no. We're taking the bike."

"But, Rob, I've never been on a motorcycle in my life."

He was delighted to hear that. "Why not?"

"I've always refused. Just as I intend to do this time. I'm not getting—"

"Chicken."

She rolled her eyes at his teasing jeer. "That's not going to make any difference. I'm not—"

"Sissy."

"Rob, I mean it, this silly name-calling is not going to make me change my mind. I won't—"

"Wimp." He stood with his hands on his hips as he taunted her, enjoying the sparks that blazed hotter in her green eyes with each successive indignity.

"I am *not* a wimp. I went up in that plane with you, didn't I? I just don't like motorcycles."

"How do you know? You've never been on one. Cream puff."

"Dammit!"

She swung at him, her fist doubled threateningly. Laughing, he caught her hand a good six inches from his stomach, as she'd obviously known he would do. He loved playing with her, loved the smile trying to hide in her silvery green eyes. He lowered his voice to a seductive murmur. "Ride with me, Brie."

She groaned. "Rob—"

He knew he was getting to her. "Please."

"All right, but if you get us killed I'll never forgive you."

"I'll keep it in mind." That was his Sabrina. She'd deny it to the end if accused, but she couldn't resist a challenge. He tugged his olive-green flight jacket off the bike and slipped it on, then reached for the helmets dangling from the handlebars. "Here. You need to wear this."

She was still frowning when he pulled the helmet over her head and snapped the smoked visor down into place. And then he pulled his own helmet onto his head, swung one leg over the bike and motioned for her to get on behind him. She did so very gingerly. He kicked the starter, pleased when her arms tightened convulsively around his waist when the powerful engine thundered into life.

"Rob?" she shouted into his ear.

"Yeah?"

"Where are we going, anyway?"

"To meet my family," he replied easily.

"*What?* Dammit, Rob, you—"

The remainder of her words, as well as his laughter, were drowned in the roar of the engine as Rob headed the motorcycle onto the street.

THEY'D TRAVELED SEVERAL miles before Sabrina actually got up the nerve to open her eyes. What she saw when she did made her immediately close them again, her arms tightening convulsively around Rob's slim waist. The problem with motorcycles, she thought as she had many times in the past, was that there was absolutely nothing between her and whatever they should happen to hit, should the worst occur. Her vivid imagination provided her with a clear image of hitting the pavement whizzing past their feet. She gulped.

"Rob?"

He didn't hear her. No wonder. This contraption made enough noise to deafen anyone. *"Rob?"*

He turned his head just enough to shout back at her. "What?"

"What happens if you lose control of this thing?"

"Double order of street pizza," he yelled cheerfully, leaning into a curve.

Groaning, she burrowed into his back and held on even more tightly, hoping she'd crack a few of his ribs. He deserved it, the fiend. He called this fun?

And what was that teasing crack about going to meet his family? At least, he had better be teasing. If he honestly expected her to meet his family with her hair flattened by a helmet, in her grubbiest clothes, then he had a lot to learn.

Some time later their speed slowed. Sabrina risked opening her eyes to find that they were entering a huge park she'd visited several times before. She relaxed just fractionally, deciding that Rob *had* been teasing about his family. He was only bringing her to a park. What a relief.

Traveling much more slowly now, they cruised the many roads of the park. Sabrina wondered where he was going. He seemed to be looking for something in particular. And then she felt him straighten in his seat as if he'd spotted what he'd been looking for. The motorcycle dipped sharply to the left and then Rob parked among a cluster of other vehicles, most of the four-wheeled persuasion.

"What are we doing?" Sabrina asked, pulling her helmet off with relief and experimentally flexing her neck. She stood tentatively beside the motorcycle, her legs a bit shaky.

"How long's it been since you played flag football?" Rob asked, climbing off the bike and hanging his helmet over the handlebars.

"You're kidding, right?"

Sliding a pair of aviator sunglasses onto his nose, he grinned at her. "Nope."

Her thoughts momentarily evaporated as her heart turned over in her chest. The noon sun caught him in full glare, gleaming off the silver at the temples of his jet black hair. His dark glasses hid his eyes, drawing her attention to his deeply dimpled smile and strong, cleft chin. The flight jacket and worn jeans made him look virile, tough, uncompromisingly masculine. He was without doubt the most beautiful man she'd ever known. And she was so close to being in love with him that she ached.

Trying to regroup her shattered thoughts, she pressed one hand to her temple and cleared her throat. "You don't really expect me to play football, do you?"

"Give it a chance, Sunshine. You'll like it." He looped one arm casually around her shoulders, holding her against him as he guided her toward a group of people milling beneath a picnic pavilion. "Hey, Mom! Look who I've brought," he called out when they were still some three yards away.

Mom? Oh, no, please. He hadn't. "Ro-ob," she wailed just as a woman in her early fifties broke away from the group and headed toward them, smiling brightly.

"Sabrina! Oh, my dear, I would have known you anywhere. No wonder Rob recognized you so quickly." Rob's

mother extended both hands in welcome, smiling at her
with Rob's bright blue eyes and irresistible dimples.

"Mrs. Davis." Sabrina was stunned to see the woman and
to recognize her without hesitation. Unlike her son, Rob's
mother hadn't changed at all during the past seventeen
years. Her hair was still dark, her face only slightly lined,
her figure still slim and attractive. Even though Sabrina
hadn't known the woman very well, she would have recognized her very quickly, if not immediately. "How nice to
see you again," she said graciously, since it was too late to
do anything about her appearance.

"Please, call me Reba. And it's wonderful to see you
again, too. How is your brother?"

"Colin's fine. He's been out of the country for several
weeks, but he's back in town now."

Reba's lovely eyes softened, her hands tightening briefly
around Sabrina's. "Rob told me that you've lost both your
parents since we saw each other last. I'm sorry. I grew very
fond of your mother during the year we knew each other."

"Thank you, Mrs.—Reba."

Still holding Sabrina's hands, Reba turned her head. "Liz!
Honey, come here. Do you remember Sabrina?"

Liz waddled toward them, her short body nearly round
in the last days of pregnancy. Sabrina searched the younger
woman's face for signs of the little girl she vaguely remembered, finding them in the still mischievous blue eyes, the
smattering of freckles over an impish nose, the reckless
smile that invited everyone seeing it to smile in return.

"Of course I remember you," Liz informed Sabrina, her
voice a pleasant alto. "You were always my favorite baby-
sitter. You treated me like a person rather than a mindless
little nuisance."

Subjecting Sabrina to a thorough scrutiny, she tilted her
dark head admiringly. "Gosh, you're even prettier than you

were as a teenager," she said with ingenuous candor. "Rob hasn't been exaggerating."

Sabrina flushed and murmured something incoherent in response, deciding she'd have plenty to discuss with Rob in private. She couldn't help wondering how Rob's family felt about him dating the woman who once baby-sat him. She couldn't help but feel uncomfortable at the realization that they must know he'd spent more than one night with her.

How could he have sprung this on her without preparation?

A short time later, Sabrina had been reintroduced to Rob's father, who looked slightly familiar but older than she remembered, and a variety of cousins she didn't remember at all. She also met Liz's husband, a pleasant, serious type who was obviously devoted to his wife and excited about the prospect of being a father.

"What is this?" she murmured to Rob at the first opportunity to speak to him in private.

"Family reunion," he drawled with that cocky grin that made her long to hit him—and then to kiss him until smoke came out his ears. "We have them at any excuse. This one's supposedly in my honor. A send-off, in a way."

"Oh." She couldn't seem to hold on to her smile at that reminder of his imminent departure. "That's—very nice of them."

He pulled off his sunglasses, his eyes meeting hers with an expression that tore at her heart. "Sabrina, I—"

A hearty voice interrupted them. "Come on, you two. Time to eat. You know if you wait too long with this crowd you just might not get anything at all."

Rob sighed almost imperceptibly and shoved his glasses back on. "Okay, Uncle Stan, we're coming. Brie?" He held out his hand to her.

Taking a deep, raw-edged breath, she hesitated only a moment before placing hers into it. She wouldn't have him for long, but for now, he was hers.

SABRINA AND ROB sat at a picnic table with his parents, sister and brother-in-law during lunch. The menu consisted of hamburgers fresh off the charcoal grill, potato salad and baked beans, the latter two items provided potluck from the various families in attendance. Cases of canned soft drinks and individually packaged cream-filled chocolate cupcakes rounded out the meal. Sabrina decided that the Davises must do this sort of thing often, as organized as the picnic was.

"C'mon, Brie, you're on my team," Rob urged, tossing an empty soda can into a nearby wastebasket as others began drifting toward the grassy stretch that would be the playing field for the traditional flag football game.

Sitting backward on the picnic table bench to watch the action, she leaned back against the table and shook her head, still lingering over her own drink. "I think I'll stay with your mother and sister for a while."

He frowned and doubled both fists on his hips. "Chicken."

Sabrina laughed up at him, refusing to allow him to manipulate her a second time. "Forget it. That won't work again."

His eyes dancing, he leaned over her, trapping her between his arms as he rested his fists on the picnic table at either side of her. "Promise you'll play during the second half and I'll let you sit out the first."

"No promises."

He brushed her lips with his. "Cream puff."

The name calling didn't bother her at all. The intensely interested scrutiny they were drawing from his family did.

"Okay, I'll play later," she promised hastily, her cheeks warm with embarrassment.

He grinned. "Great."

"Rob! Come on, we're ready to kick off."

Without turning his head, he yelled an acknowledgement of the summons, "Be right there."

And then he lowered his voice for Sabrina's benefit. "See you later." He kissed her again before he turned to lope toward the family members—male and female from ages of about ten to fifty—waiting on the grassy playing field.

Sabrina kept her gaze on Rob for the next few moments as she cleared her throat and tried to will away the blush staining her cheeks. She could feel two pairs of speculative eyes on her during the silence that followed his departure.

"Um—how have you been feeling, Liz?" Sabrina asked hastily, leaping on the first topic that came to mind.

Her amused eyes telling Sabrina she'd recognized the diversionary tactic for what it was, Liz patted her stomach. "I'm getting impatient now that the due date's only a few days away. I can't wait to hold him in my arms."

"Him?" Sabrina smiled at the younger woman's rapt expression.

"Or her. Rob's gotten me into the habit of saying him. He's so sure the baby's a boy."

"He's very excited about becoming an uncle," Sabrina commented in amusement. "I was with him when he bought out half of Baby World the other day."

"He's driving me crazy, accusing me of deliberately waiting until after he leaves to go into labor. He has no idea how ready I am to get this pregnancy over with."

"I can imagine."

"It really is nice to see you again, Sabrina," Liz murmured after a moment. "We have so much to catch up on. You never married?"

The bluntly asked question put Sabrina on guard for a sibling-type interrogation, but she answered politely, "Yes, I was married right out of college, but it only lasted a few years."

"Oh." Liz watched her husband as he ran a few yards with the football before being tagged. "I guess you were surprised to run into Rob after all these years. He told me you didn't recognize him."

"No, I didn't. That's not surprising, though. He's changed a great deal."

"He has, hasn't he? I've always said he was the one with all the looks in the family. Funny, when we were kids I thought he was a pest, but now that we're both grown I'm crazy about him."

"I feel the same way about my brother."

"Rob *is* special, though," Liz continued. "He's honest and bright and talented. Sweet-natured, too, and so loving. He's just good, you know?"

Sabrina nodded, touched by Liz's obvious adoration of her older brother, but wondering where the conversation was leading. "I'm aware of that, Liz." That, and more, she thought.

Liz seemed to grow tired of skirting issues. "So what's going on with the two of you?"

"Liz," Reba murmured warningly, giving her daughter a reproving frown.

Liz flushed. "It's just that I was so surprised when he told me he was seeing you and he—well, he's spent quite a lot of time with you."

"Believe me, Liz, I'm as surprised by this as you are," Sabrina said with a heartfelt sigh.

"Okay, then let's forget all about this awkward little talk and watch the game, shall we?" Liz said brusquely.

"I think that's an excellent idea." Reba sounded relieved, leading Sabrina to suspect that Liz's forthright manner had caused her mother embarrassment on more than a few occasions.

Though her attention was outwardly on the game for the next half hour, Sabrina couldn't help worrying about the purposes behind that "awkward little talk." Was Liz, like Sabrina, worried that Rob was putting too much expectation into a boyish infatuation, afraid he'd be hurt when it failed to survive reality? And, having acknowledged exactly how wonderful Rob was, couldn't Liz understand that Sabrina was the one who'd be devastated when he was gone?

The remainder of the afternoon passed quickly. Finally coaxed into the game by Rob and his family, Sabrina played hesitantly at first. And then her natural competitiveness and determination took over and she threw herself into the action with the same vigor as the others. She couldn't remember laughing so much or having more fun in a very long time.

Rob's father passed her the ball and Sabrina sprinted toward the goal, heedless of the grass stains on her knees and the strands of hair that had long since escaped the braid and now flew around her flushed face. The red "flag" tucked into the back waistband of her jeans was the target of the other team—pulling it out constituted a "tackle." She dodged one of Rob's younger cousins, a twelve-year-old girl with a determined look on her freckled face and a blue flag hanging from her own waistband.

The goal was only a few feet away when a solid weight hit her from behind. She went down like a rock, landing on top of her assailant, who had twisted beneath her to take the impact of the fall. Winded and indignant, Sabrina glared down into Rob's gleaming eyes as he lay beneath her, arms wrapped around her, laughing. "Unfair! This is flag football, not tackle! I demand a penalty call."

"Blame my dad. He's the one who got greedy and claimed you for his team instead of letting me have you on mine."

"That's a very weak excuse for breaking the rules and tackling me," she retorted haughtily, uncomfortably aware of the intimacy of their position and the fascinated attention they were getting from the various members of his large extended family.

"You're right," he assured her gravely, his low-pitched voice meant for her ears only. "The real excuse is that I wanted a chance for a quick feel." He slid one hand lower on her back.

"Rob!" Blushing furiously, Sabrina shoved herself off him just as his father—her team's captain—descended on them with cries of foul over the illegal tackle. Rob was banished to the sidelines for the next three plays and Sabrina returned to her own team, but she was well aware that his eyes rarely left her. Just as she found herself looking at him more often than at the football.

All in all, she thought with a grim attempt at humor, her plans for having a subtle, discreet affair with the man were slowly disintegrating. There was nothing subtle about the way Rob had behaved today.

Quite an interesting man, this Rob Davis, she thought as she sat on the sidelines, catching her breath after a player change. She watched as he playfully wrestled with two adolescent boys, then bent to dry the tears of one of the youngest players who'd fallen and bruised his knee. He obviously loved children. Remembering the way he'd looked earlier that day in his aviator glasses and flight jacket, so young and cocky and handsome, she tried to think of one word to describe him. The dated term "cool" was the only one that seemed to fit. He was self-confident, easygoing, seemingly unshakable, except where she was concerned. With Sabrina, he was vulnerable, a little uncertain at times, sensitive about his age.

But was she so different? At her office Sabrina was firmly in control, her emotions hidden behind a facade of strict professionalism. Only with Colin, Angel, Mandy and a few of her close friends had she allowed her softer side to show— until Rob had come along and opened all the secret doors with only his smile. The heart she had protected so diligently for so long was completely exposed to him.

She'd never felt more vulnerable, or more resigned to inevitable pain, in her entire life, not even when she'd realized her marriage would not succeed.

SABRINA WAS GRUBBY, windblown and nearly exhausted by the time Rob guided the motorcycle into her driveway and turned off the noisy engine. The leave-taking from his family had been lengthy, with numerous hugs and cheek-kisses, warm invitations for her to join them again, plenty of subtle and not-so-subtle probing into her relationship with Rob from his many aunts and cousins. But she'd still enjoyed the day very much, despite her initial reservations.

Rob kept an arm around her shoulders as she unlocked her door. "You were great today, sweetheart. You had the family eating out of your hands."

"I can't believe you took me to a family reunion without a word of warning. I was ready to strangle you earlier."

"And now?" he asked, closing the door behind them.

She smiled faintly and turned into his arms, loosely clasping her hands behind his neck. "Now I'm open to suggestions."

His own smile was brilliant. He kissed her lingeringly. "As a matter of fact," he murmured, his lips still brushing hers,

"I was just about to suggest that we go upstairs and—uh—rest from all that strenuous exercise."

Sabrina opened her mouth to wholeheartedly agree, but was interrupted by a voice from the kitchen doorway. "Before this conversation gets really embarrassing, I think I'd better warn you that you have company."

Sabrina whirled out of Rob's arms. "Colin!" she cried, spotting the lanky redhead lounging amusedly against the kitchen door frame. In the next minute she was across the room, being hugged enthusiastically to her younger brother's rather bony chest. "Oh, it's so good to see you. Where's your car? I didn't notice it outside."

"The son of a gun wouldn't start. I think it's sulking because I left it alone for six weeks." Colin shrugged, studying his sister's glowing face. "You look terrific."

Sabrina grimaced, knowing exactly how disheveled she was. "You're the one who looks wonderful. I can't believe how tanned you are for a redhead." She examined his face approvingly, then playfully pinched his rib cage. "Still too skinny, though. Didn't they feed you at all in Africa?"

"Yeah, but don't ask what they served. You wouldn't want to know." Colin transferred his attention to the man who stood silently watching them. "This must be Rob Davis."

"Yes." She turned to Rob, who seemed to be concentrating on scratching behind Angel's ear as the dog all but sighed in ecstasy. "Rob, you remember Colin?"

"Of course," Rob answered politely enough, though his voice was curiously expressionless. He extended his hand. "Good to see you again, Colin."

Gripping the proffered hand, Colin looked Rob up and down before shaking his head in amazement. "I never would have known you. Last time I saw you, you were a runt of a kid, and now you've got three inches and at least thirty pounds on me. I hope you're not going to challenge me to a fight this time."

Rob smiled, his cool expression thawing a little as he obviously remembered the incident to which Colin referred. Sabrina remembered it, too. Rob had lit into Colin with a small boy's healthy fury after Colin had once startled Sabrina with a garden snake. "That depends on whether you frighten your sister again." He looped a casual arm around Sabrina's shoulders, pulling her to his side.

Her cheeks warming at the speculation in her brother's eyes, Sabrina shot Rob a warning glance before asking, "Can I get you guys something to drink?"

"I was just looking for something when you came in. Don't you have anything stronger than fruit juice?" Colin complained. "I've had a hard day."

"I'll look."

Colin nodded and dropped into a chair, stretching his long legs out in front of him. Angel curled up at his feet and rested his chin on Colin's ankle, obviously comfortable with Sabrina's brother.

"Rob?"

"Juice will be fine. Need any help?"

"No, thanks. Sit down and talk to Colin. I'll be right back."

He moved to the couch, settling with masculine grace into the deep cushions. As she left the room, Sabrina heard him say, "Brie tells me you're a free-lance photographer, Colin."

When she returned with the tray of drinks, Colin was describing the book he'd been commissioned to illustrate in Africa. Sabrina settled beside Rob on the couch. He lounged back against the cushions, seemingly at ease, but with a revealing hardness in the muscular arm he again draped around her shoulders. She sensed the tension in him and felt a small satisfaction at so neatly turning the tables on him by having him unexpectedly meet a member of her family. She wondered if it bothered him that Sabrina's younger brother was still three years older than Rob. And then she squirmed uncomfortably and decided to change the subject.

"So where's my present?" she asked her brother, trying to make her smile look as natural as possible.

Colin grinned at Rob. "I've spoiled her. She thinks I have to bring her a present every time I leave town. I think it's because she's still got wanderlust in her own veins and travels vicariously through me."

Rob looked contemplatively at Sabrina, who only shrugged. "Think whatever you like," she said casually. "Just give me my present."

Chuckling, Colin reached down to the floor beside his chair, coming up with a rectangular white box. Sabrina smiled sweetly at him, then ripped into the box eagerly, making both men laugh. The caftan inside was batik dyed in a bright yellow-and-green pattern. "Colin, it's lovely," she exclaimed, rising from the couch to kiss him. "Thank you."

"You're welcome. They come in every color imaginable, but I knew you'd like that one."

"Rob, isn't it beautiful?" She held the floor-length garment in front of her for his inspection.

"Beautiful," he agreed huskily. He wasn't looking at the caftan.

Sabrina flushed.

"Would you look at that—Brie's blushing!" Colin announced with the tactlessness of a sibling. "Haven't seen that in years."

Exhaling her exasperation, Sabrina quickly changed the subject. Colin could certainly be annoying at times—like all younger brothers. And Rob, well, there was no doubt that Rob carried a chip on his shoulder about certain things, all of them concerning her, it seemed. When had her life gotten so complicated? she wondered. And then she answered her own question. It had happened the day Rob Davis had strolled into an elevator and into her life.

"Well, as interesting as this has been, I guess I'd better call a cab," Colin announced a few minutes later. "My girlfriend's expecting me."

"I'll give you a ride if you don't mind riding on the back of a motorcycle," Rob offered.

Colin's brows shot up in surprise. "Brie's been on a motorcycle?"

"Yes, I have."

"Amazing."

She refused to comment, saying instead, "You can take my car, Colin. I'm not planning to go anywhere else tonight. Casey can follow you back here later tonight to drop it off."

"Thanks, I'll do that. And thanks for the offer, Rob."

"No problem."

Sabrina tossed Colin her spare keys, which she'd retrieved from a small cherry secretary in one corner of the room. "I'm glad you're home, Colin."

"Good to be home." He hugged her quickly.

Rob reached the door ahead of Colin. "I'll go move the bike. It's parked behind Brie's car."

Colin lingered for a moment after Rob went outside. "That guy's crazy about you, Sis," he observed, watching her expression as he spoke.

She bit her lower lip, his words adding to her concern about Rob's expectations. She decided to wait until later to tell Colin about Rob's overseas assignment. She really didn't want to get into her strange relationship with Rob just now.

Colin was watching her face. "You kind of like him, too, don't you?"

She smiled weakly. "What's not to like?" she murmured, though she didn't share the private joke with him.

"He's done some weight lifting since we saw him last, hasn't he?"

"Yes. I noticed that right off."

He chuckled. "I had a feeling you did. Thanks for letting me borrow the car."

"Sure. Just leave the key in the glove compartment when you drop it off. I've got mine on my key ring," Sabrina murmured. Then, chewing her lower lip, she mechanically stroked Angel's sleek head as she stared after her brother.

Rob came back into the house, tilting his head at the expression on Sabrina's face. "Something wrong?"

She shook her head. "No, of course not. Would you have recognized Colin as quickly as you did me?" she asked lightly, unwilling to share her worries with him.

"Yeah. He hasn't changed much. A little taller and skinnier, but that's about it." He caught her around the waist to pull her closer. "Kiss me, Brie."

She complied willingly. The kiss lingered for a very long time. And then Rob pulled back with a wicked sparkle in his bright blue eyes. "Now where were we when your brother so insensitively interrupted us?"

"I think we were going upstairs to *rest*."

He nodded. "Yeah. That's what I remembered." Without warning, he swung her up into his arms, high against his chest, and headed for the stairs. "How about we share a shower first?"

She laughed a protest—not at his suggestion, but at his actions. "Rob! Put me down. You're no Rhett Butler, remember?"

"I've always wanted to try it."

Wrapping her arms around his neck, she snuggled trustingly against his shoulder. She didn't tell him that being carried up that flight of stairs fulfilled a secret fantasy of her own.

11

SABRINA WOKE to Rob's kiss Sunday morning. It was quite a while before they got out of bed. They cooked breakfast together, laughing and teasing, stopping frequently for a kiss or a touch. Refusing to think of anything serious, Sabrina spent the day enjoying his company. She intended to relish every moment with Rob even if it killed her. And sometimes she thought it might. Because behind every bright smile, every happy laugh, every passionate embrace lay the painful knowledge that time was sweeping past her. It was as if a clock in her head had begun to tick, counting down the minutes until Rob was gone.

After an almost idyllic day, they came perilously close to a quarrel Sunday evening. It rained steadily all day, but the weather only made their time together more intimate. They made no attempt to step outside. Settling onto her couch with coffee after dinner, they tried to watch television, though their attention kept wandering to each other. Sipping her drink, Sabrina studied his face from beneath her lashes and wondered how it was possible that he'd woven himself so deeply into her life in such a short time.

Catching her gaze, Rob smiled, set his cup down on the coffee table and reached out to touch her cheek. "It's been another great weekend, hasn't it?"

She rubbed her cheek against his knuckles. "Yes," she murmured. "A wonderful weekend."

Rob lowered his hand to his thigh, suddenly looking rather uncomfortable. "I have a confession to make."

She raised an eyebrow. "What confession?"

"I woke up restless in the middle of the night, couldn't get back to sleep. I didn't want to disturb you, so I left the room and I read the rest of your book. Well, what you've written so far, anyway."

She set her coffee cup on the table so abruptly that the beverage splashed over the sides. "Dammit, Rob! You had no right to do that without asking."

He looked faintly apologetic, but his strong jaw set stubbornly. "I know I had no right to ignore your wishes, but I couldn't resist. Your writing is so good, Brie. You pulled me into the story and then held me there till I finished reading. I can't understand why you try to hide this talent of yours."

"Look, I told you. It's only a hobby for me. Even if by some miracle I had a chance of getting published, I—"

"Of course you'd be published," he interrupted firmly. "You're damned good."

"And you may be just a shade biased," she accused him, though some of her anger dissipated at his words. It meant so much to her for him to praise her writing. More than she could have imagined. And yet it made her uncomfortable, too. Rob was already so much a part of her life. Now he'd even invaded her last private dream. How could she possibly put him out of her heart, when there was no part of her he hadn't touched, hadn't left his mark upon? "You're no expert on publishing, Rob."

"No," he admitted. "But I know good writing. And I know that publishers are always looking for talented new writers. And," he added flatly, "I know you've never given up that dream of writing, no matter how vehemently you may deny it."

She looked away from him. "You're wrong."

"I'm right. I know you, Brie."

"You only think you know me," she murmured. "A few months when we were kids, the past two weeks. That's not enough time to really get to know someone."

"Isn't it?" His voice was gritty.

"Obviously not. I'm happy with my life as it is, with my business and my friends. Why can't you accept that?"

"You deserve so much more," he said.

"Don't do this, Rob. Not tonight. Please." She hated the weakness in her own voice, the raw pleading that almost hinted at panic. She could almost hate him for making her feel that way. Almost. If only she hadn't so foolishly fallen in love with him.

"Sabrina, I—" He bit off the words, his eyes dark with emotions she couldn't begin to understand. And then he drew in a deep, unsteady breath and gave in. "All right. We won't talk about it anymore tonight. But soon we have to talk. You know that, don't you?"

She closed her eyes. "I'm not sure there's anything to talk about," she whispered. "You'll be leaving soon and I—I'll go back to the way things were before."

He reached for her so abruptly that she tumbled into his lap. His hand clenching in the hair at the back of her head, he lowered his mouth until he muttered against her lips. "You won't forget me, Sabrina. Every time you laugh, every time you dance, every time it rains—dammit, every time you look at another man, you'll remember me."

And he kissed her until she thought she'd pass out from lack of oxygen. Until she no longer cared whether she did. And for the first time she realized that Rob Davis could be cruel. Because he had to know that every word he'd just spoken was painfully, undeniably true.

He left soon afterward, telling her he'd talk to her the next day. Sabrina sat alone in a chair in the silence, so very much aware of her solitude, of the quiet he'd left behind him. The only sound she heard, above the steady rain and the occasional rumble of thunder, was the inexorable ticking of that hateful mental clock.

HIS ARMS FULL of packages, Rob followed his sister into her home Monday afternoon. "You buy anything else for the nursery and there's not going to be room for the baby. You know that, don't you?"

Liz smiled over her shoulder before lowering herself carefully into a chair in her contemporarily furnished living room. "I've got to have something to do until the baby gets here. I'm going crazy waiting around."

Heading toward the hallway, Rob smiled back at her fondly. "The doctor said any day, right? It won't be much longer."

"I hope not."

"I'll dump this stuff in the nursery and then I've got to make a phone call. You need anything first?"

"No, thanks. I just want to put my feet up for a few minutes."

"Give a yell if you need me. I'll be in the den."

Stopping by the brightly painted nursery only long enough to toss his sister's purchases into the yellow enameled crib, Rob veered straight to the den, eager to talk to Sabrina. Dropping onto the deep leather couch, he pulled the extension phone into his lap and dialed her office number, which he'd already memorized.

"Dial-a-Temp."

"Hi, Julia, it's Rob Davis. Is Sabrina busy?"

"Yes, she is. She's conducting an interview."

"Damn. Do you know how long it'll take?"

"Another fifteen minutes or so, I'd imagine. And then she's scheduled for another one, though the applicant hasn't arrived yet. Would you like me to have her call you when she gets a minute?"

"Yes, please." He gave her his sister's number. "Tell her I'll be here most of the afternoon, okay?"

"I will. Oops, there's the other line. It's been a real madhouse here since noon." And she hung up almost before Rob could respond.

Disappointed that he hadn't been able to talk to Sabrina, he set the phone back on the table and stood, heading without much interest toward the kitchen. "Want a cup of tea?" he asked his sister as he passed the doorway to the living room, where she still sat leafing through a magazine.

"I thought you were going to make a call."

"Brie was busy. Her secretary's going to have her call me back here."

Liz set the magazine aside, studying her brother in concern. Rob frowned impatiently, already aware that Liz was worried about his involvement with Sabrina. She'd made that clear enough during their shopping outing that morning, asking too many questions for which he had no good answers. To forestall any more of them, he hurriedly asked again if she wanted tea. "How about some of that raspberry herbal blend you like?"

"I'll make it."

"Hey, that's why I'm here, remember? To take care of you on the housekeeper's day off. Better take advantage of it. If you weren't in such a delicate condition, I'd have you waiting on *me*."

Liz snorted her response. He continued to tease her as they walked together to the kitchen, choosing to avoid the subject of Sabrina for the moment. There were times when his younger sister was entirely too perceptive.

Rob and Liz were in the den, watching a cable television program on baby care when the telephone rang over an hour after his attempt to reach Sabrina. He nearly sprawled on his face in his eagerness to answer the phone. Aware of Liz's rather disapproving expression, he deliberately turned his back on her, smiling when he heard Sabrina's voice. "Busy afternoon, huh?"

"Very," Sabrina agreed, sounding tired. "I had two interviews and then we got a call about an accident involving one of our temps."

"An accident?"

"Yes. She fell over some equipment at the office where she was working. She cracked a couple of ribs, but I was assured that she'll be fine after a few days of recovery."

"Do you carry workers' compensation insurance for the people who sign up with you?"

"Of course. And the rates continue to skyrocket," she replied with a sigh. "Of course, there may prove to be negligence involved here on the part of the office where Cassie was working today. It's being investigated."

"Your work sounds very—um—interesting," he commented, without much enthusiasm. Actually, the temporary employment field did sound interesting to him, but he just couldn't imagine Sabrina spending a lifetime in it. Thinking of the book she was writing, he wondered if she'd ever have the nerve to try the writing career he suspected she'd truly love. On a more selfish note, he'd like to see her try writing because that career would make her more mobile. She could write anywhere.

Germany, for example.

"Yes, it can be. I enjoy working with different people and the challenges that crop up so often."

"I'm sure you do. Listen, Brie, about tonight."

"Yes."

He ran his fingers through his short-cropped hair. "I'd forgotten that I promised my best friend from Irving that

I'd have dinner with him and his wife while I was in town. Pete Slater, do you remember him?"

"No."

He winced. "No, I—uh—guess you wouldn't." He'd forgotten for the moment that he and Pete had been five years behind Sabrina in school. Her clipped answer told him that she hadn't forgotten. *Smooth move, Davis.* "Anyway, tonight's when I'm dining with them. Will you go with me?"

She hesitated, then spoke slowly. "I don't think so, Rob, but thank you for asking me."

"Come on, Brie, it'll be fun. You'll like Pete and Rosie. They're a great couple."

"I'm sure your friends are very nice, but I'm already rather tired and I still have a long afternoon ahead of me before I can leave for the day. Tax reports are due—it's April, you know—and I've got several more calls to make. I've got to talk to the insurance agent, too, about this accident today. By the time I can get away from here I'll be ready to go home and collapse."

Sensing that Sabrina was only telling half the truth with her list of excuses, he still knew he couldn't change her mind. The thought of not seeing her, even for one day, left him feeling hollow, particularly when he thought of how little time he had left to spend with her. "All right. Will you see me tomorrow night? I'll buy you a steak dinner."

"That sounds nice. I'd like that."

He smiled again. "Great. I'll call you tomorrow then, okay?"

"Yes. Enjoy your visit with your friends."

"I'd enjoy it more if you were with me."

She remained quiet, letting the hint pass.

Resigned, he gave in. They talked only a couple of minutes longer before Sabrina told him she had to go. Rob was frowning when he replaced the receiver.

He turned to find his sister watching him steadily.

"You're going to be hurt, Rob. You're getting too involved this time." Her face was grave with her concern for him.

"What makes you think that?" he tried to ask lightly.

She refused to be put off. "I know you. And I can read the look in your eyes. You've fallen hard this time."

She didn't know the half of it, he thought grimly. If Liz knew that Rob was hopelessly in love with Sabrina Marsh, she'd really have reason to worry. Because he was. Deeply, totally, permanently in love. And he had no reason to think his love was destined for a happy ending. "Why do you automatically assume I'm going to be hurt?" he asked anyway.

Her mouth twisted wryly. "You're on your way out of the country, remember? You planning on conducting a romance from thousands of miles away? Or do you think there's a chance that Sabrina's going to walk away from her career and her home to follow you to Germany?"

"Is that so inconceivable?" he asked quietly.

"Oh, Rob." Liz leaned forward as much as her awkward shape allowed and grabbed his hands, holding them tightly. "Don't do this. Don't let yourself start hoping for things that are so unlikely to happen."

He drew in a deep, sharp breath. "What if I told you that I was thinking about asking her to marry me?"

Her blue eyes went liquid with fear. "You've only known her—what? Two weeks?"

"Something like that. But it doesn't matter. I knew almost from the first that she was the woman I wanted for my wife."

"Oh, dammit, Rob, I *knew* you'd do this someday!" Liz cried out despondently, dropping his hands to wring her own in her nonexistent lap. "Why do you always have to throw yourself into commitments with everything you've got? You've done it with flying, with the air force and now with Sabrina. Your family worries about all the time you spend in dangerous flight situations, we hate having you taken away from us for months and years at a time by your job and now I just know you're going to have your heart broken by Sabrina Marsh. When are you going to learn to be more careful about the situations you hurl yourself into?"

Rob's mouth twisted in exasperation. "Would you stop being so melodramatic? I'm a damned good pilot, a careful pilot. I like my job and have enjoyed the traveling so far. As for Sabrina, well, I didn't fall in love with her on purpose. It just happened. There wasn't time to consider the consequences. If it doesn't work out—" He cleared his throat before finishing the sentence. "If it doesn't work out, I'll survive."

"But at what price?" Liz whispered.

At the price of one permanently damaged heart, Rob could have told her. He didn't. Instead, he shrugged fatalistically and shoved himself off the couch. "I think I'll go take a shower and change. Pete's expecting me in a couple of hours."

MONDAY EVENING found Sabrina wandering aimlessly around her home, touching things. Things that reminded her of Rob. The chair he'd sat in, the rinsed cup in the sink that had held his coffee, the pillow that had cradled his head during the nights he'd slept with her. Odd how the place had never seemed so empty before when she was home alone with Angel.

She tried to work, but couldn't concentrate. She tried to read, but the love scenes in the novel reminded her too painfully of Rob. Finally, she went upstairs to her typewriter, spending an hour with the novel she'd denied writing until Rob had proven differently. But then even that failed to stop her thoughts from drifting back to Rob.

He'd changed everything, she thought in near panic. He'd insinuated himself into her life before she'd had time to bolt her emotional gates against him. *What now?*

He'd turned her life upside-down. Made her begin to believe in that passionate, intense, soul-shattering love again that she'd long since stopped hoping to find. Hadn't she known all along that if she ever started to dream again, those dreams would bring nothing but pain, as they always had in the past?

She moaned at her own stupidity and hid her face behind her hands. Concerned by her behavior, Angel whined and rested his head on her knee. Sabrina sighed, dropped her hands and slipped her arms around her pet's thick, warm neck. "Oh, Angel. What am I going to do?"

SABRINA HAD half-expected Rob to be waiting for her when she arrived home from work Tuesday. He wasn't. She hadn't heard from him since that unsatisfactory telephone call the day before, though she'd expected him to call all day. She was intensely aware of his absence when she entered her home, automatically returning Angel's greeting. Two weeks earlier the dog's affectionate welcome would have been enough. Tonight the rooms all seemed empty. Rob wasn't there.

"I'd better get used to it. He leaves next Tuesday," she said out loud, her words falling heavily into the silence. She snapped on the stereo, dialing to a rock-and-roll station to drown out the deafening silence. Wondering where Rob was, she climbed the stairs, pulling off the jacket to her green linen suit and tugging at the collar of her white silk blouse. She didn't even know what time to expect him for their dinner date.

Slipping into her red kimono, she wandered restlessly downstairs, perching on the edge of a chair as she absently patted Angel. "I don't suppose he told you what time he'd be here this evening?" she asked the dog whimsically.

Over an hour later she was pacing, her arms crossed tensely. Where was Rob? How could he waste the few hours they had left together? Had something gone wrong?

So this was what it would be like when he was gone, she thought, her stomach going hollow with a pain that threatened to swallow her.

Some time later she heard a noise outside her door. She had the door open before he even had time to ring the bell. "I wasn't sure you were coming tonight," she said, trying to keep her smile relaxed, her voice casual.

He entered with a broad smile, dropping a kiss on her lips before pressing a Polaroid snapshot into her hand. "I'm sorry I'm so late. I got delayed. Check this out."

Biting back a rush of questions she had no right to ask, Sabrina glanced down at the photo. It took a moment for the significance to strike her. Her eyes widened at the picture of the newborn baby sleeping in a hospital nursery bed, tiny fists curled against his chest. "Rob! Is this Liz's baby?"

Beaming proudly, he nodded. "My nephew. Born a little over two hours ago. Eight pounds, ten ounces. I tried to call you when he was born, but I'd just missed you at your office and you weren't home yet so I decided to wait and tell you in person."

"Congratulations, Uncle Rob." Rising on tiptoe, she kissed him. "I missed you when I got home," she couldn't help admitting. "I've gotten kind of used to having you here."

"I've gotten used to being here." He hugged her fiercely, then set her back a few inches, smiling down at her. "Want to go meet the newest member of my family?"

"Of course. Come up and talk to me while I change. When did Liz go into labor? Did she have a hard time? Aren't you thrilled that the baby was born while you were here?"

"Slow down," he said with a laugh, following her up the stairs. Sprawling onto the end of her bed, he made himself comfortable as he watched her dress and tried to answer all her questions at once. "Liz went into labor at about ten this morning while she and I were having coffee. Gordon met us at the hospital at just before noon. Mom and Dad joined us an hour later. Liz came through beautifully and yes, I'm delighted that I was here for the big event."

His eyes narrowed when Sabrina slipped off the kimono to reveal a creamy teddy. "Come here a minute."

She laughed knowingly at the expression on his face and shook her head. "I'd better not. We should go on to the hospital before visiting hours end." Ignoring his growl of protest, she slipped into a bright plaid shirtdress.

"One kiss?" He held out his arms in invitation.

"One kiss," she agreed, walking over to sit on the bed beside him. She tilted her head toward him, surprised when he put up a hand to stop her. "What is it?"

"I think I'd better come to you," he murmured, climbing to his feet. "If you get on this bed with me now, we won't be leaving until morning."

And then he kissed her with a hunger that shook her all the way to her soul before determinedly setting her away. "If we're going," he said hoarsely, "we'd better leave now."

JONATHAN GORDON HOLLEY was completely indifferent to the visitors who'd gathered to welcome him to the world. Curled into a little ball, he slept, his tiny fists curled, a bewildered frown crinkling his baby face. Sabrina and Rob agreed that he was the most beautiful baby in the nursery, to the proud delight of his parents and ecstatic grandparents. Liz was tired, of course, so they didn't stay long. They walked back to the nursery window on their way out of the hospital. Glancing away from the baby, Sabrina noted that Rob's expression was distant as he looked through the glass. She wondered if he were imagining what it would be like to be in Gordon's shoes.

She wondered why she was suddenly feeling so sad, so empty at the thought of never having a child of her own. Hadn't she convinced herself that she'd long since come to terms with that probability?

Catching her gaze, Rob smiled and announced, "I'm about to pass out from hunger. I haven't eaten since breakfast."

"Well, we can't have that, can we?" Sabrina returned with enforced cheeriness. "I'll buy dinner to celebrate the birth of your nephew."

"You're on." Catching her hand, he walked with her to the elevator. As they stepped through the doors, he murmured, "Liz and Gordon looked very happy, didn't they?"

"Yes," she agreed quietly. "They did."

He kept his eyes on the control panel as he pressed the lobby button. "They're very lucky."

"Yes." Her voice sounded rather strained coming from her tight throat. "Very lucky." And she, too, looked away, not wanting Rob to see the hopeless, wordless longing she suspected would be reflected in her eyes.

After they made love that night, Sabrina lay staring at the ceiling while Rob slept beside her. Something was keeping her awake. Perhaps it was the sound of the clock ticking away their time, growing louder as the hours passed. She put her hands over her ears to drown out the sound and tried to will herself to sleep.

ON WEDNESDAY NIGHT Rob and Sabrina double-dated with Colin and his girlfriend, having dinner at one of the newest "in" places in Dallas, followed by a trip to one of Colin's favorite noisy clubs. A kindergarten teacher, Casey was a pretty, dark-haired, bubbly young woman who, at twenty-three, had always made Sabrina feel vaguely dull and settled. She'd half-teasingly scolded Colin for getting involved with someone so young, accusing him of doing so deliberately to make his sister feel older. She took a long time to get ready for the evening, worrying about what to wear, painfully aware that she'd be the oldest one in the group. She couldn't help thinking that Casey was much more suited to Rob than Sabrina was. She couldn't help wondering if he would think so, too.

She needn't have worried. Rob made it clear that he had eyes for no one but Sabrina, though he seemed to like Casey well enough. Blossoming under the warmth of his smile, Sabrina found herself laughing and teasing and chattering as easily as the others.

It was getting quite late when Colin turned to Sabrina. "I'd like to dance with my sister."

Rather surprised, Sabrina glanced at Rob, who smiled and nodded. "Go ahead." He turned to Casey. "Would you like to dance?"

"I'd love to." Casey placed her hand in Rob's. Sabrina watched them disappear onto the dance floor without the concern she may have felt earlier that evening. Perhaps the smile Rob sent back over his shoulder to her had something to do with her complacence.

Stepping into her brother's arms for the beginning of the dance, she tilted her head to look up at him in question. "Why the sudden urge to dance with your sister?"

He made an absurd effort to look innocent. "Do I have to have a reason?"

"Don't you?"

Colin only shrugged. "I just wanted to dance with you, okay? It's been a long time since we danced together."

"Yes," she murmured, unable to even quite remember the last time. "I guess it has."

Colin was silent for a moment, his lean body moving gracefully to the strains of the romantic song. And then, his eyes trained intently on her face, he asked, "He makes you happy, doesn't he?"

She'd expected this. Phrasing her answer carefully, she replied, "I enjoy being with him. He's a lot of fun."

Colin's mouth twisted. "It's more than that. You're crazy about the guy. I've never seen you look at anyone the way you look at him."

She kept her eyes trained on the collar of his dark green shirt. "I'm—very fond of Rob. Call it a temporary infatuation."

"Why don't I call it what it really is? You're in love with him."

Sabrina sighed, wishing for once that her brother didn't know her quite so well. "Okay, so maybe I am. But I'll get over it."

"Are you sure?"

Her smile felt bitter. "It won't be the first time, will it?"

"I think it may be," Colin answered slowly, thoughtfully. "This one's different, isn't he?"

"Colin, please. Not now."

He sighed and pulled her more closely into his arms. "I just want you to be happy, Brie. I want you to keep smiling the way you have tonight. I don't know if I can take seeing you hurt again."

Touched, Sabrina pressed her cheek to his. "I'm a survivor, remember?" she whispered. "I'll be fine."

"I want you to be more than fine. I want you to be happy."

"I'm happy tonight," she answered gently. "That's enough for now. Don't spoil tonight, Colin."

He sighed, obviously wanting to say more but unable to argue with her request. "All right. But if you need to talk—"

"I know. And thanks."

The song ended. Colin hugged her briefly, then released her, only to catch her wrist when she would have turned and walked back to the table. "Brie?"

"Yes?"

"There's no chance that you and Rob—" He hesitated, trying to find the right words.

She didn't give him time to finish. "Rob leaves for Germany Tuesday. He'll be there for two years. He has no choice but to go, and he's never indicated that he'd rather stay, even if he could."

"But maybe the two of you could still see each other sometimes. Write, call, you know."

"A long distance affair?" She shook her head. "Can you see a healthy young man like Rob being content with that type of relationship?" And knowing that he was seeing other women while she lived from one letter to another would kill her, Sabrina added silently. When Rob left, it had to be permanent. That was the only chance she had for ever getting over him.

Colin pulled Casey onto the dance floor for one last dance before the evening ended. Following suit, Rob drew Sabrina into his arms, seeming pleased that another slow number followed the last. He looked at her searchingly. "You and Colin seemed very serious during your dance. Is something wrong?"

She shook her head, reveling in the feel of his arms around her, his strong, warm body moving against hers. "No. We were just talking. Did you enjoy your dance with Casey?"

He nuzzled her cheek. "She's very nice. But I'd rather have been with you." And then he whispered exactly what he'd have liked to do with Sabrina.

Clinging to him as her knees went weak, Sabrina promised in a husky murmur that he could do every one of those deliciously naughty things with her as soon as they were alone. And that she had a few ideas of her own.

Rob's eyes glowed with his approval just before his mouth covered hers.

12

THERE WAS TO BE a reception Thursday evening for the members of the local Personnel Managers Association. Sabrina belonged to the group, as did Katherine and other personnel directors, employment agency and temporary service owners. Feeling obligated to attend, she'd hesitantly asked Rob if he'd like to join her. He'd readily accepted.

Standing quietly in the background, Rob watched Sabrina work the cocktail party that evening, mingling with her associates and counterparts in the personnel management business, subtly drumming up business for her service. Dressed in a dark evening suit, her hair in a sleek roll at the back of her head, she fit right in with the professional group. Laughter was restrained, smiles polite, conversation low-voiced. Though he assumed most of the people in the room were more relaxed away from a professional environment, it was particularly hard to imagine Sabrina as the same woman who'd played flag football with his family less than a week before.

Serious. No-nonsense. That would be the only Sabrina these people would know, he realized, other than Katherine, who'd been allowed glimpses of the warm, witty, caring woman beneath the facade Sabrina had learned to project sometime during the past few years. Very few people truly knew her. Colin, Mandy. Who else? And did anyone but him know the depths of passion lying beneath that cool, unruffled exterior?

How could she possibly be happy subduing her personality all the time to fit the mold she believed most suited to her position?

It broke his heart to think she'd go back to a life of all work and little play when he left. That the brilliant smiles he'd seen more and more often the past few days would fade again into these polite, restrained smiles she was wearing tonight. He clenched his fists in the pockets of his suit, resisting the urge to do something crazy—like throwing her over his shoulder and hauling her out of here, taking her someplace far away where it could be just the two of them. Forever.

"Give me a call tomorrow," Sabrina told the short, balding man in front of her. "I'm sure Arlene will be exactly what you're looking for to fill in during your secretary's maternity leave. She's one of the most efficient and competent employees on my staff."

"I'll do that," Walker assured her, then turned his head toward the bar. "I believe I'll have another drink. How about you?"

"No, thank you. I'd better get back to my friend."

Sabrina crossed the room slowly, nodding at a few people she knew, giving a quick smile to Katherine as they passed each other. Poor Katherine. The president of the organization had her by the arm, no doubt trying to convince her to head a committee or secure a speaker for the next monthly meeting.

Her heart beating just a bit faster, she drew closer to Rob, hungrily studying his handsome face as he watched her approach. He looked...distant, she thought. Withdrawn. Was he bored? He looked almost sad.

And then his expression cleared and he smiled and held out his hand to her. "How's business?" he murmured.

"Moving right along," she replied. "Are you very bored?"

"Oh, no. I've found it quite interesting watching you tonight."

Sabrina frowned at something she heard in his voice, but before she could question him the crowd was urged to take their seats in the meeting room for the evening's program. A state senator would be speaking on a controversial employee benefits plan that would be proposed to the legislature soon. Normally, Sabrina would have been very interested in hearing what the senator had to say. Tonight she only wished the meeting was over so that she and Rob could be alone again.

They had so little time left.

TWO HOURS LATER they were finally alone at her house. At Rob's request, Sabrina made coffee. "Would you like some cookies or something to go with that?" she asked him as she handed him his mug.

"No, just coffee." Leaning against the kitchen countertop, he carefully sipped the hot beverage and watched as she poured a cup for herself. Angel sniffed at his feet, obviously hoping to be slipped a treat. Rob patted the dog's head in an absent gesture that indicated his thoughts were otherwise occupied. "Did you enjoy tonight, Brie?" he asked unexpectedly, his eyes oddly intense.

She shrugged. "It was okay. Pretty much routine."

"You seemed very comfortable there."

Curiously wondering where his questions were heading, Sabrina nodded. "Comfortable? I suppose so. My work involves a lot of evenings like that."

"All work and no play, Sabrina?"

She winced. "Usually," she agreed quietly, setting her cup on the counter and staring down at it.

"You deserve more." His voice was little more than a gruff murmur.

"Don't start this again, please. I've told you that I'm content with my life. You're the one who seems to think there's something missing."

His own cup hit the countertop with a force that sent coffee sloshing over the rim. "Isn't there?"

She sighed and closed her eyes. "I don't know anymore. You confuse me, Rob. I—I feel—"

He stood close behind her, his hands closing gently around her forearms. "What do you feel, sweetheart?"

"Like—" She tried to think of an analogy. "I feel like a quiet, sober little town and you're the circus, just traveling through. While you're here there's music and laughter and excitement and fun. When you're gone, my life will go back to the same as it was before, but I can't help worrying that I won't be the same. That I'll always be aware of the empty place you occupied for just a little while."

His fingers tightened convulsively on her arms. She kept her eyes closed, afraid that she'd revealed too much with her blurted answer.

"Brie," he murmured, his voice husky. "It doesn't have to be that way, you know. We can make the excitement last."

"How?" she whispered, though she was afraid of his answer.

"Marry me, Sabrina. Go with me to Germany."

Whatever Sabrina had expected, it hadn't been that. She gasped and whirled out of his grasp to face him, her eyes feeling huge in her face. "*Marry* you? Are you serious?"

Rob flinched. "Hell, yes, I'm serious!" he growled. "That's hardly something I'd joke about."

She groped for the counter behind her, suddenly needing something to hold on to. "I—I don't know what to say."

His eyes softened, his voice going deep, persuasive. "Say yes, Brie. I love you."

Her heart convulsed in pain. "Oh, Rob," she moaned. "You hardly know me. You're in love with a memory, with a boyhood infatuation. You can't—"

He cut her off with a word she'd never heard him use before. And then he stopped and drew in a deep, unsteady breath, as if reining in his temper before he continued. Eyeing him warily, she realized she hadn't even known he had a temper—not like this.

"Don't tell me what I feel," he said, his words very evenly spaced, very deliberately enunciated. "I am *not* a boy and this is *not* a boyhood infatuation. I've been attracted to other women, formed a few tentative relationships in the past, but I've never felt like this. I'm in love with you. I think I fell in love with you in that damned elevator. Every moment I've spent with you since has only made me love you more."

"Rob, I—"

"You don't still think of me as an immature kid," he told her flatly. "Dammit, you couldn't. Not now."

"No, of course I don't."

He looked relieved. "Then you don't really believe that what I feel for you is a boyhood infatuation, do you? You were just saying that because I startled you with my proposal. I guess I shouldn't have blurted it out so bluntly, but—well, it's just that our time is running out. How can I convince you to go with me when I leave Dallas."

"Rob, please. Don't," she moaned. "I can't go with you. Can't you see that? I have a life here, I own a business, a home. I can't just walk away from it all on the basis of a three-week-long affair."

His eyes flared again. "This is more than just an affair, Sabrina. It was always more than that, from the very beginning. I love you."

She crossed her arms tightly over her chest and dug her fingers into her forearms to hide her trembling. "I'm sorry." The words were only a whisper.

"You love me, Sabrina. Dammit, you have to love me," he added fiercely. "You wouldn't have made love with me so honestly, so passionately if you didn't love me. That's not your way."

Her trembling increased until she was leaning against the countertop to keep from crumpling to the floor. "Maybe— maybe I do," she admitted. "I don't know anymore. If the timing had been different, if you weren't on your way out of the country, maybe we could have worked something out, eventually."

His eyes narrowed, his jaw working. "Really? Or would you have been forced to find another excuse to avoid committing yourself to me?"

"I don't know what you mean."

"You're a coward, Sabrina Marsh. You've been hurt a time or two, so now you're hiding from real life behind the carefully constructed make-believe life you've built for yourself. The woman who attended that party tonight, the woman I first saw in that elevator—she's not real. She's a caricature of a modern career woman, with no real feelings, no dreams, no aspirations. The Sabrina I love is a real, warm, loving person longing to break out of the walls she's built around her. You're a dreamer, a writer, Sabrina—a passionately alive woman you've never managed to fully subdue.

"You're the one who said you were afraid your life would seem empty when I'm gone," he went on relentlessly. "I can tell you—it will. It'll seem empty and lonely and cold, because it *will* be empty and lonely and cold. What you and I have found together doesn't come along every day, Brie. It's a once-in-a-lifetime thing that most people only dream of finding. We could have a family, a lifelong commitment, a chance at making all our dreams come true. I'd give anything to hold on to what we have. If I could stay here with you, I would. Unfortunately, mine isn't the kind of job where I can just call and give two weeks' notice. I can't just quit. But if you turn this opportunity down, if you deliberately walk away from it, you'll spend the rest of your solitary life regretting it. I just know you will."

She'd thought once before that Rob could be cruel. Now she repeated that thought as her heart slowly bled from the wounds he inflicted.

Even knowing that his words were prompted by pain and bruised pride, she lashed back out at him. "Look, I was perfectly happy with my life before you came into it. I have no intention of giving up everything I've earned to follow you around the world. I've had enough of dreamers and drifters. I need a home, the security of knowing that I have my own life to turn to, my own place. I can't go back to just being someone's wife, my identity hinging on your rank or your success. That's not enough for me now."

"You're comparing me to your first husband?" he demanded incredulously. "Don't you know I'd never treat you the way he did? Nor would you ever allow yourself to fall back into that kind of rut. You have too much spirit, too much imagination and ambition for that."

"Then what do you *think* I'd do in Germany? Open a temp service in a country where I don't even speak the language, knowing you could be transferred somewhere else at any time? I don't think so."

"My God, Brie, the possibilities are endless. You'd be in Europe. What better place to begin your writing career?" He paused for emphasis, then added more tentatively, "And if we had children, we'd both have plenty to do when we weren't working."

The thought of having Rob's children made her feel like crying, but she blinked back the tears. "Oh, Rob," she said sadly. "Writing is an old dream I gave up a long time ago. You have to let it go, too. You've got an exciting time ahead of you. You'll find someone else—"

"Dammit, Sabrina!" Furiously, Rob reached out for her, obviously intending to pull her into his arms and kiss her until she listened to him. He stopped abruptly when Angel, disturbed by the tension in the room, moved protectively to Sabrina's side, a low growl sounding in his massive chest.

Rob stood very still, staring at the dog, his face devoid of expression. And then he lifted his eyes slowly to Sabrina's. The pain there brought the hot tears back into her eyes to trickle down her cheeks. Rob was hurt almost as much by Angel's defection as by Sabrina's.

"He's trained to protect me, Rob," she felt compelled to whisper. "Even against people he likes."

"Yeah." Rob pushed his hands into his pockets and looked away. "Maybe I'd just better go now. I think we both need some time to think."

Without looking at her again, he turned and strode rapidly away, a young, wounded animal restlessly searching for a place to be alone with his pain.

Though the tears continued to roll, Sabrina was able to prevent herself from breaking into sobs by the force of will. She knelt on the floor beside Angel, stroking and soothing the agitated animal. Her first impulse was to call Rob back. The front door slammed and she knew it was too late. Why had she let him walk out that way?

She knew why. She'd been acting like a lovesick teenager since Rob had first reentered her life. She'd allowed Rob to rush her into a date, into bed, into love, without giving her time to stop and look at what she was doing. Now he was asking her to give up everything she had achieved in the past few years—her career, her home, her independence—to follow a man she'd known for only a matter of days!

He was a dreamer. A self-proclaimed dreamer who found nothing foolish in the sacrifice he asked of her. A man like her father, who'd blithely pursued his own lofty dreams at the expense of his family.

No. She forced herself to be honest. Rob wasn't exactly like her father. True, they were both dreamers, but Sabrina's father had been a weak man, easily led astray. He hadn't even had the conviction of his dreams, abandoning one for another as easily as some people changed clothing. Rob wasn't weak. He was the kind of man who set his sights on his goals and let nothing distract him until he achieved them, no matter how impossible they may seem to others. If he hurt anyone along the way, it wouldn't be intentional.

But Sabrina couldn't afford to dream. Maybe she was a coward, but she was so afraid of reaching out again, risking another failure. She'd never thought she'd be able to deal with the rejection that was an integral part of a writing career. And she'd avoided romantic relationships lately because she hadn't wanted to fail again in that part of her life. She'd worked so hard to make a success of herself, of her business. It had been a timorous, unadventurous life, perhaps, but she'd been content with it.

She couldn't do it. No matter how much she loved Rob, no matter how desperately she wanted him, she couldn't risk so much for him. He was asking too much. He was asking for everything she had to give.

Finally she started to cry, unable to swallow the sobs any longer. It wasn't fair! If only she hadn't left work early on that Tuesday afternoon, if only she hadn't been in that particular elevator at that particular time. Her life had satisfied her before Rob had come into it. Now she knew she'd never be quite satisfied again, not without him. Her days before had been full, busy; now there would be a gaping void that should have been filled with love and laughter and joy—with Rob.

She remembered the months after her divorce. She'd been bitter and angry and sad, but she'd never felt as though a part of her had died. She would feel that way when Rob was gone, because there was a part of her that had never been alive until he'd brought it to life.

"It's not fair," she whispered, her watery cheek pressed to Angel's sympathetic neck. "Dammit, it really isn't fair."

DESPERATELY NEEDING TO talk to someone, Sabrina called Katherine the next day and asked her to meet her for lunch. Sensing the unhappiness in her friend's voice, Katherine agreed immediately.

"You look like hell," were her first words when Sabrina dropped into the booth opposite her in the quiet restaurant they'd agreed upon.

"Gee, thanks, Katherine. I needed to hear that." Sabrina pushed dispiritedly at her hair as she stared down at the salad she didn't want.

"What's wrong?"

"Rob asked me to marry him."

Katherine choked. "No kidding?"

"No. He wants to get married now. Wants me to just drop everything and follow him to Germany." She spread her hands on the table in front of her, palms up. "Can you believe that?"

Reaching across the table, Katherine took Sabrina's hands in hers. "It is a lot to ask, isn't it?"

"Too much," Sabrina agreed, her throat painfully tight.

"You've fallen in love with him, haven't you?" The question was quietly sympathetic.

Sabrina briefly closed her eyes. "Is it that obvious?"

"It is to me. I've known you quite a while."

"Yes, I love him. Do you think that's stupid after so short a time?"

"No. I don't think it's stupid at all." Katherine paused, then asked carefully, "So you told him no?"

"Of course I told him no! Katherine, I've known the man less than three weeks. I can't just run off to Germany with him. What would I do there, sit in a tiny base apartment all day? Join the Officers' Wives Club? Some women might be content with that, but I wouldn't. I was the football hero's wife and when that marriage ended I didn't know who the hell I was. I've worked so hard to build my own career. I can't just throw it all away on a romantic whim."

"How long will Rob be in Germany?"

"He's tentatively stationed there for two years."

"That's not so long," Katherine suggested hopefully. "He'll be home on leave a time or two, won't he? And you could always fly to Germany for a vacation. And there's always the mail and the phone lines."

Sabrina shook her head. "I've already discussed this with Colin. I don't think either Rob or I are the types to carry on a long-distance relationship. I'd be too insecure and he—well, he wants to get married now. He wants to start a family. In two years, I'll be thirty-five years old."

"Big deal, I'm thirty-five now and I could certainly have children if I wanted to."

Sabrina shook her head. "I just can't see Rob living in celibacy for the next two years, even if things did work out for us at that time. And I couldn't bear to share him. It would be easier to give him up now. I've been that route before, too. It's too painful."

"What's it going to be like when he's gone, Sabrina? Is your career going to be enough for you then?" Katherine asked gently, her eyes sharing her friend's unhappiness.

The wave of pain that swept through Sabrina almost made her gasp. "No," she answered starkly. "It won't be enough. I want it all, and I can't have it."

"I wish there was something I could do to help you."

Sabrina tried very hard to summon a smile. "You've helped by letting me talk to you. I really needed that today."

"Any time. Just remember I'm here when you need me."

"Thanks. I think I'm going to need you a lot in the next few weeks."

AS SHE HAD SUSPECTED he would be, Rob was waiting for her when she got home that evening. He was sitting in his car at the curb when she pulled into her driveway. Before she could get out of her car, he was at the passenger door, sliding into the seat beside her. "Let's go someplace quiet where we can eat dinner and talk."

"Is that supposed to be an invitation?" Sabrina asked dryly, her hands clenching on the steering wheel to keep from touching him.

"That's the best I can do right now. I'd suggest we go inside, but I'd just as soon not be mauled by your dog while I'm trying to talk to you."

She turned the key in the ignition, restarting the engine. "Where do you want to go?" she asked, ignoring his bitter remark.

"I don't care. Anywhere as long as we can talk there."

Sabrina chose a nearby Mexican restaurant where the booths were given a semblance of privacy by a profusion of green plants. She and Rob ordered margaritas with little enthusiasm, both aware of the tension hovering between them.

Rob smiled a thanks at the waitress who'd brought their drinks in a remarkably short time. When he and Sabrina were alone again, he cradled the large frosted glass between his hands and stared into its salt-rimmed depths. "This was the longest day of my life."

"I know the feeling." She took a deep swallow of her drink.

"I guess I don't have to ask if you thought about what happened yesterday." He slanted a glance at her through his short, dark lashes.

Sabrina laughed, but the sound bore little resemblance to humor. "If only you knew how hard I tried to think of anything else."

Drawing a deep breath, Rob spoke quickly. "Sabrina, I've been thinking. I know I rushed things yesterday with my proposal. You weren't ready, you're still not, and I can understand that. It's just that—well, it didn't take me long to know what I wanted with you. I hoped you felt the same way."

"Rob, it's not that I'm not honored by you asking me to marry you. I am, very much. If only you were staying in Dallas—but you aren't. And what you asked was too much."

"I know that now," he answered grimly, but not without sympathy. "I guess I was expecting too much." His mouth twisted. "I meant what I said yesterday, you know. If I could call the air force and say 'Look, guys, I'm sorry, but I've fallen in love and have to quit,' I would. But I have a recently renewed four-year contract to fulfill, Brie. I can't just walk away from it."

"I wouldn't ask you to. Flying is your life. I know that."

He hesitated only a moment before saying softly, "Flying was my life before I met you. Now you are. I'd quit if I could, if it would change things between us."

"Dammit, Rob!" Sabrina stopped to regain control of her volatile emotions, reminding herself they were in a public place. "Don't you know what you're saying? A relationship based on sacrifices like that could never work. You'd end up hating me for everything I'd cost you."

Rob reached across the table to take her hands in his, shoving their drinks heedlessly out of the way. "I hear what you're saying, Brie. You think I'm obsessed with you and you're right, I guess. I've never been in love like this. I never even thought I *could* love like this. I could never hate you."

Leaving her hands quiescently in his, Sabrina stared at him, torn and confused. "You really think you could give up everything without regrets?"

"I didn't say there wouldn't be regrets," he answered gently. "I'd miss flying terribly. But not as much as I'll miss you next week. And the week after that, and all the weeks after that."

How could he sound so confident, she wondered wildly. Could he possibly love her that much? And then she pulled her hands from his as the truth occurred to her. Of course Rob could speak with such assurance. After all, to him it was only a hypothetical question. It was her career in jeopardy, not his. "I'm sorry, Rob."

"Yeah." The word was tinged with a bitterness he couldn't quite conceal. The waitress stopped by their table for their dinner orders, which they placed with barely a glance at the menu.

"You really like your job?" Sabrina asked after a long moment of strained silence. "You don't find service life too restricting?"

"I haven't. Not until now. It's a good life. I've made a lot of friends and have had opportunities in aviation that wouldn't have been possible in a civilian job. I'd like to join the Thunderbirds eventually—"

"The Thunderbirds?" Sabrina interrupted to repeat in surprise, thinking of the air force flying team that had been delighting crowds at air shows for years with their heart-stopping stunts. Their very dangerous heart-stopping stunts, she added, her throat tightening at the very thought.

He smiled rather sheepishly. "Yeah. *My* dream," he explained. "But even if that never comes through, I'd still planned to stay in the service until retirement. I'll be eligible to retire at forty-two."

"Fourteen more years," she murmured. "Fourteen years of never knowing where you're going to live next? Never knowing what you'll be called upon to do?"

"I don't think you really want to discuss the political or patriotic aspects of my career just now, do you?"

"No, not really," she answered with a sigh. Either way it would be difficult—if not impossible—for her to be with Rob and still own her own business. Not at the risk of being reassigned with him at any time.

Their food arrived and for a while the two unhappy lovers sat in silence, pretending to eat. And then Sabrina glanced up to find Rob watching her, his dinner abandoned. "I love you, Sabrina," he murmured.

His words brought tears. Sabrina blinked them back rapidly, praying she could get out of the restaurant without disgracing herself. "Let's go, Rob. Please."

Rob threw a handful of bills on the table and rose to escort her. Outside, she handed her keys to him and slid into the passenger seat of her car. Rob climbed beneath the wheel, then turned to her, studying her in the dusky purple twilight, oblivious to the people passing the car. "I mean it, Sabrina. I love you."

With a broken sob, Sabrina turned blindly into his arms. "Don't, Rob. It hurts so much already."

"I know," he whispered, holding her tightly, his face against her hair. "It's going to kill me to leave you."

"I'll miss you. I'll miss you so much."

He inhaled sharply and drew back. "I'll take you home."

Sabrina had her tears under control by the time he parked the car in her driveway. "Invite me in," he murmured, one hand against her cheek. They both knew he wasn't asking for a cup of coffee.

"It won't—it can't change anything, Rob."

"I know. But I want you tonight. I need you tonight, Brie."

How could she send him away? Nodding, she reached for the door handle.

Rob kept a protective arm around her as they walked the short path to the front door. Inside, Sabrina ordered Angel to stay behind as she and Rob walked unhesitatingly toward the stairs. They went up side by side, bodies brushing, heads close together.

Their lovemaking was silent, frantic, desperate. Each sought a release from the pain their impending separation brought. Neither found it. Lying in his arms afterward, Sabrina remembered when she had wished to freeze time. Now she wished she could turn the time back to that one beautiful moment.

Rob stirred beside her. "It doesn't end when I leave Tuesday. You know that, don't you?"

She drew a quick breath. "Rob—"

"I mean it, Sabrina. I'm not going to stop loving you just because we aren't together. I'll love you until the day I die. I won't stop trying to talk you into marrying me, even if I have to wait four more years and settle in Dallas to convince you that I'm not an irresponsible drifter."

"I think it would be better if we end it now. Easier on both of us," she forced herself to say, though she wanted to call the words back as soon as she'd spoken them. "I can't possibly ask you to—"

"You're not asking me to do anything," he broke in flatly. "I'm telling you. I'll write, I'll call, I'll be here whenever I have a few days' leave. I'm not giving up on us, Sabrina. What we have is too important to me."

"I don't know what to say."

"Are you going to refuse to see me when I'm here? Hang up on me when I call? Return my letters unopened?"

"Of course I'm not going to do any of those things," she whispered, knowing better than to think she could be that strong. She didn't really expect to have to resist him for long. He was young, his sexual drive strong. It wouldn't be long before he found someone else. Someone more available. Someone who'd know better than to let a man like this get away.

"I've made a commitment to you, Sabrina," he startled her by saying, as if he'd read her thoughts. "I'm in love with you. You're the only woman I want."

"I certainly don't expect you to be celibate during the time we're separated," Sabrina told him, the words so very hard to say.

"Well, I'm damned well going to expect you to be celibate, so you may as well ask the same thing," he answered hotly. "Dammit, Sabrina, you love me. I want to hear you say it. Just once, I want you to be brave enough to tell me the truth."

"I—" She closed her eyes, unable to lie to him now. "All right, I love you. But—"

He covered her mouth with his, kissing her deeply, lingeringly. "I only wanted to hear you say it," he murmured, holding her tightly. "I love you, Brie. Do you think it's impossible for a man to be faithful to the woman he loves? Did your experience with an unfaithful husband completely ruin your faith in men?"

"No, of course not. But we'll be separated for so long."

"You went for a lot longer than that without sex, didn't you? And it wouldn't be the first time I've gone for a long time, myself. When I left my teens, I decided I'd be very selective with relationships and I have been. I've always known there would be one woman I'd want to dedicate my life to, and I was right. I've found that woman in you."

She smiled sadly, wanting so desperately to believe him, unable to put her faith in his beautiful words. She wouldn't hold him to a commitment made in the heat of passion, she told herself. She'd give him time away from her and then they'd both see just how lasting his love would be.

And then she lost herself in his kiss, telling herself that just for the remainder of the night she could pretend that they'd never have to say goodbye.

13

SABRINA WAS INVITED to dinner with Rob's family on Sunday evening. Had there been a graceful way out, she would have declined. As it was, she couldn't bring herself to disappoint Rob again. He seemed to want her there very badly.

Since Liz was only recently out of the hospital, the dinner was held at her home, though Reba served as hostess. Sabrina dutifully admired tiny Jonathan, taking him gingerly into her arms when Liz offered to let her hold him. "He's beautiful," she murmured, eyes fixed on the tiny features. She thought the baby looked a lot like his uncle Rob. Perhaps her child would look like this, if . . .

But no. She couldn't start thinking that way. Such thoughts were too dangerous, too painful. She glanced up from the baby to find Rob staring at her, his eyes reflecting her own thoughts. And she wondered if it were possible to be any more miserable.

"I'll go finish dinner. It should be ready in a few minutes," Reba announced, heading for the kitchen.

"By the way, Rob, my car was making a funny sound on the way over here," Rob's father commented, his expression amusingly sheepish. "Maybe you'd better go look at it for me before I head back home."

"What kind of a sound?"

His father shrugged. "Ker-chunk, clang, ker-chunk."

Rob rolled his eyes. "How can a man who's such a genius in business be so inept with anything mechanical?" he asked the room at large.

"To each his own talents," Liz defended her father.

Rob slung an arm around the older man's shoulders. "C'mon, Dad. I'll show you how to open your hood."

"I'll come with you," Gordon said, joining the two Davis men. "I want you to show me what a spark plug looks like, Rob," he added teasingly.

Left alone with Sabrina, Liz walked slowly over to the couch, her comfortably loose tropical-print dress swaying around her. "I'm not up to my usual speed yet," she explained with a grimace as she lowered herself to the cushions. "Damn, I'm sore."

Sabrina smiled, cautiously transferring the baby to his mother's arms. "Here, you'd better take him now. And I think you're doing great. You look wonderful."

"You wouldn't believe how much smaller I feel," Liz said with a grateful sigh. "I'm not back into my jeans yet, but I'm getting there. I was beginning to wonder if I would ever see my toes again."

Sabrina laughed and reached over to stroke Jonathan's downy head. "Don't tell me it wasn't worth it."

"It was. Every nauseous, bloated, back-aching moment." Liz kissed the baby, then looked through her long lashes at Sabrina. "Rob told me that he proposed to you," she said, abruptly changing the subject.

Sabrina tensed. "Did he?"

"Yes. I understand why you said no, of course. I mean, you've only known him a few weeks and you have your life here and all. But he really loves you, Sabrina. He's hurting."

"I know he is," Sabrina whispered. "I'm sorry."

Liz sighed and reached out to pat Sabrina's hand. "He's not the only one, is he?"

"No. He's not."

Her eyes unhappy, Liz squeezed Sabrina's hand before releasing it. "If there's anything I can do... If you ever need to talk..."

"Thank you," Sabrina murmured, touched by the offer.

Liz nodded. And then the men returned and Reba announced that dinner was ready. Sabrina tried hard to enjoy the rest of the evening, though it wasn't easy. She sensed that her pain and Rob's was shared by everyone in the room.

The evening ended early. Rob took Sabrina home, then proceeded to spend the night making love to her. Over and over, each time making her promise she wouldn't be saying a permanent goodbye to him when he left on Tuesday. Lost in the magic of his lovemaking, willing to suspend her doubts for that one more evening, Sabrina promised she wouldn't be the one to end their relationship. Not yet, anyway.

And the clock ticked on.

SABRINA WAS twenty minutes late getting to work Monday morning. It had been harder than ever to leave Rob, knowing as she did that there would be only one more night with him. She clasped the anticipation of that night to her, comforting herself with the reminder that there would be those few last hours to hold him, love him, pretend again that she'd never have to let him go.

Then she looked up from her work just before noon to find Rob standing in the doorway to her office, his face grave, his eyes so very sad. And somehow she knew the idyll was already over.

She'd never seen him in uniform before. The neatly tailored blue jacket and slacks looked wonderful on him, his shirt collar crisply starched, his tie precisely knotted, two shiny silver bars proclaiming his rank. He held his cap in his hands, but she could picture it sitting correctly on top of his head. And as handsome as he looked in the uniform, she still resented it bitterly, knowing it was taking him away from her. "What's wrong?"

"I had a call this morning. A friend of mine was killed in a midair collision over New Mexico last night."

Her hand flew to her throat, which had tightened both in empathy with his pain and the reminder of how dangerous his job really was. "I heard about that on the car radio this morning! I had no idea, of course, that one of the men killed was a friend of yours. Were you very close?"

Lines of repressed pain bracketed his mouth. "We were at the Academy together. Yeah, we were very good friends."

She stood and walked around her desk to lay her hand on his arm. "I'm so sorry," she said weakly, wishing there was something more she could say, something she could do to help him.

Rob took a deep breath and shut the door, giving them privacy. And then he drew her farther into the room and looked at her. "I have to leave, Brie. Today."

Somehow she'd known and yet still his words lanced her heart. She placed a hand over it as if to hold the pain at bay. "Today?" she repeated in a whisper.

He nodded. "The funeral's Wednesday. I've been asked to fly the missing man formation with four of Tom's other pilot friends. I couldn't say no. I need to go out early to see his widow and to make the necessary arrangements."

"Of course," Sabrina agreed, though she really wanted to scream a protest at having those last few precious hours ripped away from her. "He was married?"

Rob's eyes were haunted. "For three years. His high school sweetheart. They have ten-month-old twins."

Tears of sympathy trembled on her lashes. "That poor woman."

Rob only nodded, unable to speak for the moment. And then he took a deep breath and glanced at his watch. "Gordon's waiting downstairs to take me to the airport. I'm leaving my car here in Dallas for now."

"I guess you shouldn't keep him waiting any longer." She clenched her hands behind her to stop them from going around his neck in an attempt to keep him with her.

Looking at her unhappily, he sighed. "The timing's never been right for us, has it?"

"No. I guess not."

A muscle worked in Rob's clenched jaw. "Walking out of this office," he said, his voice hoarse, "is going to be the hardest thing I've ever done in my life."

He looked young and heartbreakingly vulnerable as he stood before her, lean and hard and tall in his uniform. Sabrina gazed at him for a long time, devouring him with her eyes, loving his dark hair, his blue eyes, his sculpture-perfect nose and devastating dimples, the tender mouth that showed the faintest trace of unsteadiness. In her mind she replayed flashes of scenes from the past three weeks—yellow balloons and candy bars, dinner and dancing, surprise flights to the coast, motorcycle rides and football, lovemaking and laughter. She wondered now if she would ever laugh again.

He stared back at her as if memorizing her face. "You're so beautiful."

She swallowed, unable to respond.

He reached out to brush his fingertips across her cheek. "You take care of yourself, you hear? Don't work all the time. Take some time off just for fun, okay?"

She managed a smile. "I will. You do the same. Watch that German beer, though. It'll go straight to the waistline."

He patted his flat stomach and tried to smile. "I'll keep that in mind. You can check me over for extra pounds next time I get home on leave."

"I'll—" She had to stop to clear her throat. "I'll do that."

"Why don't you go see Liz every now and then? I'd like for the two of you to be friends."

"Maybe I will." But she knew she wouldn't. It would be too painful to see Rob's family without him there.

Rob inhaled deeply and ran one hand through his short hair. "I guess I'd better go. It's not going to get any easier."

She stood on tiptoe to kiss him. "Please be careful."

His arms closed around her. "I will. I love you."

"I love you, too." She wondered if it would be the last time she'd tell him. She knew it would never stop being true.

His kiss was hard, lingering, hungry. He ended it with obvious reluctance. "See you, Brie," he muttered, stepping away.

"See you, Rob," she whispered, almost inaudibly.

He crossed the room to the door. His hand on the knob, he turned back for one last look at her. The anguish on his face destroyed her self-control.

"Oh, Rob." Flinging herself into his arms, she broke into sobs. "I'll miss you."

"Sabrina," he groaned, holding her close, his strong arms trembling. "God, it hurts to leave you."

"I can't stand it," she gasped, the words torn from her throat in an impetuous rush. "I'll go with you. I'll pack quickly, I'll close the office, I'll—"

Rob groaned again and pushed her face into his shoulder, muffling her words. His voice was raw when he spoke. "Oh, sweetheart, you don't know how hard this is for me to say, but I can't let you do that. I can't let you go with me in a moment of panic. You had your reasons for turning me down and I don't think you've changed your mind, not really. You have to be sure. You have to know exactly what you want. No rash decisions you may only come to regret later."

Tears streamed down her face, dampening his jacket. "I thought you were the one who promised I'd never regret marrying you."

"I don't think you would," he answered huskily. "But you have to believe that as well. From the beginning."

"Rob—"

"No, Sabrina, please. Don't do this to us. It's just making it harder." He set her away, not meeting her eyes. "I have to go," he choked, turning to fling open the door.

And then he was gone.

The clock had stopped.

SABRINA LEFT THE OFFICE early for the second time that month. Numb, she rode the elevator down, trying not to remember that last time she'd left early, that elevator stop that had brought Rob into her life.

Cocooned inside her house, she cuddled with her endlessly patient pet, her grief too deep even for tears. She didn't eat, she let the answering machine pick up any calls, she wouldn't have answered the door even had anyone rung the bell. No one did.

That night she dreamed she was wandering through a large, empty lot. A circus had been there. The area had been crowded with people, resounding with music and squeals and laughter. Now it was silent, deserted. The only signs that the circus had ever been there were the scraps of colored paper fluttering at her feet. She'd never felt so very much alone.

Her own low moans woke her. She spent the rest of the night staring at the ceiling, dry-eyed, aching, her heart feeling as empty as the abandoned lot in her dream.

She finally gave up on sleep and crawled out of bed, an hour earlier than she usually rose. Sipping a cup of coffee, she stared blindly out the window over the kitchen sink, dimly aware that she had cramps. Great. Just what she needed. That time of the month. She and Rob had been very careful to take precautions against pregnancy, but now even that depressed her. She wondered if she shouldn't have been less cautious. Since she couldn't imagine ever loving anyone else, and since she didn't expect her relationship with Rob to survive even a few months of separation, her last chance at motherhood had probably passed her by. Her heart ached for the black-haired, blue-eyed baby she would never hold.

And still she couldn't cry.

She dressed for work in one of her favorite outfits, hoping it would lift her spirits somewhat. She was on her way out the door when it occurred to her that the bright blue jacket she'd paired with a crisp white skirt was almost the exact color of Rob's eyes. She thought of changing. Then she told herself she was being ridiculous and walked out the door, hardly sparing a glance for the heavy gray clouds overhead. They seemed to suit her mood.

The rain began before she even made it to her office building, coming down in torrents that made it hard to see the road. Parking in her usual space, she reached beneath the seat for the umbrella she kept there, knowing it would provide little protection from the downpour. She was right. By the time she made it into her building she was soaked.

She worked with the efficiency of a computer, carefully concealing any signs of the pain that never went away. Julia and Beverly gave her many sympathetic looks, but Sabrina ignored them, deliberately discouraging any talk about Rob. Katherine and Colin both called during the day; Sabrina requested that they give her time before asking any questions about her ill-fated romance. Because they loved her, because they sensed the extent of her suffering, they did as she asked, both assuring her they'd be around when she needed them.

Colin, particularly, was concerned since he would be leaving in only a few weeks for a new photo assignment in Greece. The thought of another goodbye—even a temporary one—made Sabrina shudder, but she hid that emotion from him as well, not wanting to worry him any more than he already was.

Rob called that night. She was already in bed, though it was earlier than she usually turned in. There'd been no reason to stay up, nothing to do that could distract her from her pain.

"I miss you, Brie."

Closing her eyes against the bittersweet ache of hearing his voice, she murmured, "I miss you, too. How are you?"

"Okay." He sounded tired, dispirited. Not at all like her happy-go-lucky Rob. "It's been pretty awful."

"Your friend's wife—?"

"Cara's holding up pretty well, considering. I think her children are the only thing keeping her going. I don't—" He broke off, sighed, then muttered, "Dammit, I don't think she's ever going to be the same again."

"How very tragic," Sabrina murmured, frustrated with the inadequacy of mere words.

"It's the first time I've faced anything like this, you know," Rob said after a long, heavy pause. "I've never lost anyone close. My grandparents all died when I was too young to realize the significance. I've never had to face suffering like this."

Sabrina's breath caught in a broken sob. His voice was so weary, older, somehow, than when he'd left. To lose a friend, to have to watch his friend's wife grieve, in addition to facing the end of his own first serious love affair—it all had hit him hard, taking away some of the almost boyish optimism, the last remnants of youthful naïveté that Sabrina had known years earlier. And she wanted to hold him so badly that her empty arms trembled. "I love you, Rob," she whispered. It was all she knew to say.

"I love you," he answered, the words choked. "Look, I've got to go. I'll call you, okay?"

He hung up almost before she could answer. Replacing her own receiver, she turned her face into the pillow and moaned softly. Was Rob crying? Was his heart breaking, as hers was? And was he even now starting to hate her for hurting him so badly?

Her silent tears turned to deep, racking sobs. It was a very long time before she finally fell asleep.

"Sabrina, you really should eat something." Katherine's attractive face was creased with concern as she looked across the table at her desolate friend.

They were having lunch again on this Wednesday in late May. Rob had been in Germany for just over a month. A month of quick, painful telephone calls, occasional letters that seemed to struggle for words. A month of determinedly busy days at work, long, lonely nights at home. She found no joy in the career she'd worked so hard to achieve; now it was only something to fill her days.

"Sabrina?" Katherine repeated impatiently. "Did you hear me?"

Startled, Sabrina looked up from her untouched plate. "Did you say something?"

"Damn, this is starting to sound familiar," Katherine muttered with a sigh. "I said you should eat something."

"Oh. I'm not really hungry."

"So what are you trying to do? End up in a hospital?"

"No, I'm—I'm just not hungry. Don't nag, Katherine." The sharp tone had been present a lot lately. Sabrina hated the way she'd been acting, but was unable to bring herself out of it. Only when she was talking to Rob did she seem to feel anything anymore, and those feelings were usually painful ones.

She took a deep breath and voiced her thoughts. "I hate this. I hate the way I'm acting, the way I feel. I hate being so damned depressed." She met Katherine's eyes. "How did I let this happen to me? I used to be so content, totally self-sufficient. Now my whole life is centered around another person and I'm bereft without him. I can't deal with this."

"Two years is a long time to suffer like this," Katherine observed quietly.

"God, do you think I don't know that?" Sabrina propped her elbows on the table and buried her face in her hands. "I keep hoping it will get better, but it doesn't," she said, her voice muffled. "How long can it take before it starts getting easier?"

"It'll have to get easier with time," Katherine predicted. "You'll get numb eventually. Then you'll see Rob when he's home on leave and you'll have to start all over again."

Sabrina lifted her head with a glare. "Oh, thanks a lot. That's just what I needed to hear."

Katherine shrugged one slender shoulder. "I'm just trying to be honest. So what are you going to do about it?"

"I don't know." Sabrina sighed and pushed her plate away. "Did you see the front page of the newspaper this morning? An air force cargo plane crashed in Italy, killing several airmen. I keep thinking, what if something like that happens to Rob?"

"Sabrina, don't. Even if you were with him in Germany, you couldn't prevent something like that if it's going to happen. Surely you know that."

"I know. But at least I'd have spent more time with him."
She rubbed at her throbbing forehead. "I don't sound like
myself at all, do I?"

"No, you don't," Katherine answered frankly.

"Maybe I should go to Rob," Sabrina blurted, eyeing
Katherine for her reaction.

Katherine shrugged again. "Maybe. But if you do, you'd
better be sure you're doing so for the right reason."

Sabrina lifted an eyebrow in question.

Katherine paused as if to organize her thoughts. "I always thought you were the most self-sufficient person I
knew. You had your own business, seemed content with
your life, your independence. You were comfortable. I
thought you were happy. And then you met Rob and I saw
what you could be like when you're really happy. You pos-
itively glowed. You always had a lovely smile, but those
earlier smiles couldn't compare to the ones you gave Rob.
When I had lunch with the two of you last month, I thought,
'There's a couple who are truly in love.' Now your eyes are
so empty and sad that it breaks my heart."

"So you're saying I *should* go to Rob?"

"Only if it's a decision you can make without hesitation,
without fear, with full confidence that you know what
you're doing and why. You can't marry him because you're
miserable without him, not if you secretly wonder if you'll
be miserable *with* him, as well. Rob's going to be gone a lot
with his job, Sabrina, and you'll have hours of your own to
fill. You're going to have to truly believe you can fill those
hours."

Sabrina had never told Katherine about her writing, nor
did she intend to now. "There is something I've always sort
of wanted to do," she admitted carefully. "But I don't know
if I can. What if I fail?"

"There's a risk of failure in everything. For that matter, you could lose your business. You know how I've always wanted to work for myself, but I've always been afraid to take the chance. Lately I've been thinking that if I'm ever going to do it, it had better be soon or the opportunity will be gone forever. You've got to want something badly enough to risk failure, whether it's marriage to Rob or whatever this other thing is you've mentioned."

"I've never realized I was such a coward. So afraid to fail again," Sabrina confessed sheepishly. "But I never had to face the kind of risk I'm facing now. My career—well, when it comes right down to it, it's only a job. But if I failed in my relationship with Rob, I honestly think it would kill me."

"Oh, Sabrina, it wouldn't kill you. You're a survivor. But you're also a winner. You put the same kind of single-minded determination into your relationship that you've put into your career and I don't think anything could destroy it."

Sabrina laughed shakily and spread her hands on the table, palms up. "That's been my major fear all along, you know. Not giving up my business or my independence, but losing Rob after having him for a while. Dumb, huh?"

"Afraid to take him for fear of losing him," Katherine mused with a sympathetic smile. "Quite a quandary."

"Yes. But it's time to stop sitting around making myself miserable. It's time to do something," Sabrina announced flatly. "I've got to come to a decision. Either to stay here and get on with my life without acting like one of the living dead or to go to Rob and somehow make it work."

"Sounds like you've summed it up pretty well."

Amazing how much better it felt just to have something concrete to do, something to concentrate on. Sabrina squared her shoulders. "I think I'll have some dessert, how about you?"

Katherine's face lit up. "I've been counting calories lately, but this sounds like as good an excuse as any to splurge. Let's do it!"

Sabrina smiled weakly at Katherine's enthusiasm, her mind still whirling with doubts and fears, longings and dreams. Yes, she definitely had to come to a decision. The most important decision in her life. She only hoped she had the wisdom and the courage to make the right choice, and then to follow through.

14

THE *GASTHAUS* looked very much as she'd expected—a noisy, crowded bar like something out of an old movie, filled with American servicemen. Some were in uniform, others in casual clothes but still identifiable by that almost indefinable something that marks one as American. Sabrina stood nervously at the door, looking around the crowded room, hoping to spot one familiar, beloved face, wondering if that would be possible.

She was so tired. It had been a long, long day. She'd begun to wonder if she'd been incredibly stupid to come all this way without calling, childishly wanting to surprise Rob. It had taken hours to track him down to this inn, which, it seemed, had become his favorite hangout during the two months he'd been in Germany.

She should've listened to Colin, who'd wanted her to call and make arrangements for Rob to meet her.

And then she spotted him. He was sitting halfway across the room at a table with three other men, all in olive-green multi-zippered flight suits. Rob's profile was to her, and it was without doubt the most beautiful profile she'd ever seen, despite the tiny lines at the corners of his mouth and eyes that seemed to have etched more deeply there since he'd left Dallas.

Her heart pounding, she stood staring at him for a long moment. She guessed there was something to the old saying that women just couldn't resist a man in uniform. But then, she'd never been able to resist Rob. *Oh, please, let him still want me. Don't let me be wrong about this.*

She twisted her damp palms together in front of her. Now that she was here, she wasn't sure what to say. He still hadn't seen her. She stood just behind his shoulder, that long-ago meeting in the elevator popping into her mind. "Excuse me," she said, tapping his shoulder, "but haven't we met someplace before?"

Interrupted in the middle of a sentence to one of his companions, Rob froze comically, then snapped his head around so quickly she worried about his neck. "Sabrina?" he whispered, staring at her in disbelief. And then, "Brie!"

His chair fell to the floor with a clatter and she was in his arms, held so tightly she could barely breathe. She didn't mind at all. Her own arms wound around his neck, her wet cheek pressed to his throat as she clung to him. How could she have gone so long without feeling his strong arms around her, his heart beating against hers?

He held her a few inches away from him so that he could look at her. "What are you doing here?"

"I seem to be out of a job and a place to live," she murmured, her heart in her throat. "I was hoping you'd offer me a home with you." *Please don't have changed your mind, Rob. Please let the offer still be open.*

She could almost see the impact of her words hit him. His eyes closed in a spasm of emotion, then opened, shining so brilliantly that she had her answer even before he spoke. "You're here for good?" he asked in little more than a hopeful rasp.

"For as long as you're here," she answered huskily. "And this time you can't accuse me of acting on impulse. I've had a lifetime away from you to think about it."

Letting out a whoop, Rob swept her right off her feet and into his arms, her toes dangling some two inches above the floor. "Hey, guys, guess what!" he announced jubilantly, looking young and cocky and so very happy. "I'm getting married!"

"Sure you know what you're doing, Davis?" one of the officers at his table asked, grinning.

Rob laughed without releasing Sabrina. His loving gaze holding hers, he murmured just loudly enough for her to hear, "Oh, yes. I know exactly what I'm doing. I've been given indisputable proof that dreams do come true."

"I LOVE YOU."

Held tightly in Rob's arms, Sabrina kissed his jaw. "I love you, too. Oh, Rob, it's been so long."

"A lifetime," he agreed, repeating her earlier words. His voice was still husky, breathing still slightly ragged as he made a massive effort to recover from frantic lovemaking that had bordered madness. "Next time," he promised, shifting more comfortably against the crisp white sheets of his bed, "we'll go more slowly."

Lying limply against his sweat-sheened body, Sabrina blinked and tried to clear her passion-clouded mind. "I feel as though I've just been whirled around in a tornado. Are you sure we didn't land in Oz?"

Rob laughed softly and snuggled her closer. "Sweetheart, we could be on Mars right now and I'd never notice. Are you okay?"

"I think so," she answered cautiously, wiggling her fingers just to confirm that she could still move. "One moment we were entering your apartment and the next we were—um—not that I'm complaining," she added hastily.

Still chuckling at her dazed expression, Rob brushed a damp strand of hair out of her face. "There are a lot of long, lonely nights in two months," he murmured. "Damn, I've missed you."

"I've missed you, too." She kissed his shoulder. "I love you, Rob."

He kissed her lingeringly, then pulled back. "Now talk. I want to know exactly what you're doing here, how you found me, what's happening to your business, your home, your dog."

"I wondered when you'd get around to asking all those questions."

"First things first," he replied with a wicked grin.

"Let's see—how did I find you," she murmured, trying to remember all his questions. "I gave this address to a very nice cab driver who spoke a little English. He brought me here and pointed out your door. When you didn't answer my knock, he took me to the other door."

Like many American servicemen who chose to live off-base, Rob was renting a small apartment in the home of a nice German couple whose children had all married and moved away. He had a tiny kitchenette and a separate entrance, all he'd required when he'd looked for a place to live.

"Frau Pischke told me about the *Gasthaus* where I'd probably find you, and she was the one who gave directions to the taxi driver. She recognized me, said you'd shown her my picture. She seems quite fond of you."

"She's a lovely woman. She's practically adopted me since I moved here, making sure I ate properly and fussing over me when I was sick. I think she's suffering from empty nest syndrome."

"You were sick?" Sabrina asked quickly, raising her head from his shoulder with a quick frown.

"Twenty-four hour flu a couple of weeks ago," he assured her. "Nothing serious."

"You should have told me when you called."

"I didn't want to worry you. Besides, I wasn't the only one holding back things during our telephone calls," he added meaningfully.

"I should have been the one taking care of you," she murmured.

"Forget that. Tell me why you're here. When and why you decided to come. Why you didn't tell me."

"I wanted to surprise you," she answered almost sheepishly. "And I couldn't tell you everything over the telephone. I wanted to talk to you face to face."

"What happened to your business?"

"I'm selling it to Katherine. She's always wanted to be self-employed and she has years of experience in personnel management. She'll do great with Dial-a-Temp. And before you ask, I'm absolutely positive I did the right thing. You were right, Rob, when you told me I'd stopped dreaming. I'd settled into a safe, unexciting life in which I had little to lose and I had grown restless with it long before you spoke to me in that elevator. I just wouldn't admit it until you shook me up and made me take a long look at what I wanted for the rest of my life."

"Your writing?"

She nodded, moistening her lips. "I brought my typewriter. And the manuscript. I'm going to finish it, Rob. I don't know if it will ever sell, but I'm going to try."

"I'm so proud of you."

Her flush deepened. "You know that the odds of selling that first book are—"

He interrupted firmly. "You'll sell it. But even if you don't, I'm still proud of you."

"I'm a little scared," she whispered, reaching out to him. The words were a massive understatement.

He understood. Capturing her hand in his, he lifted it to his lips. "I know, sweetheart. You've really gone out on a limb, haven't you? Just remember that I'll always be beside you, to support you when you need me, to cheer your accomplishments. To love you. I'll always love you."

"I was afraid, before, of loving you because I worried about losing myself again, having my own identity lost behind yours. Now I know that I am my own person, with my own dreams, my own goals, my own strengths. But I'm stronger than I was before, because I have you, too."

He smiled tenderly. "That's what you had to understand, Brie. I've always known that you were more than a title, more than a career. Just as I'm more than the silver bars I wear or the pilot's license I carry in my wallet. We're two strong, capable, ambitious people who just happen to need each other. It doesn't make us weaker, or less than we are. It just makes us human."

"So wise," she murmured, touching his cheek. "I love you, Rob."

"Ah, Sabrina." He leaned over to kiss her deeply, then pulled back to stroke her cheek with one unsteady hand. "I was so miserable without you."

"You couldn't possibly have been as miserable as I was. I made everyone around me miserable," she admitted in embarrassment. "When I told Julia what I was going to do, she cried. And then I called Katherine, and she cried, too. It was her idea to buy my business, though I'd already wondered if she might be interested. Then I told the O'Neals—Ellen cried, too—and they're buying the duplex. I gave Angel to Mandy—"

"You did *what*?"

"I gave him to Mandy," she repeated, her smile a bit wistful. "She's devoted to him, you know. The entire family is. They'll take very good care of him."

"Sabrina, you loved that dog."

"Yes," she agreed softly. "And I thought this was best for him." She took a deep breath. "Anyway, Colin's storing my furniture for me until I decide what I want him to send here. I don't think I'll need much of it. Oh, and I called Liz and your mother just before I left. They—"

"Don't tell me," Rob broke in comically. "They cried."

Sabrina laughed and nodded. "Yeah. But they seemed pleased."

"Do you know that you've made me the happiest man alive?" Rob asked conversationally, his hands warm around hers.

"I want to spend the rest of my life making you happy," she whispered around a large lump in her throat. "I want to help you make your dreams come true, just as I know you'll help me reach for mine."

"Even if my dream is to fly to the stars?" he asked with a crooked smile.

"I'll be waiting to welcome you when you come home," she returned decisively. "Maybe our children will be standing beside me."

He pulled her roughly into his arms and buried his face in her hair. "Oh, God, Sabrina. I couldn't ever be happier than I am right this moment. I love you so much."

"I love you, too." Her hand crept down to stroke his thigh.

"Don't ever leave me again."

"I didn't leave you. You left me, remember?" She trailed one finger through the crisp dark hair on his muscular leg.

"Then don't ever send me away again. Not like that."

"Never." Her fingers moved inward.

Rob sucked in his breath. "Sweetheart, what are you doing?"

"You know. You said we'd go slowly next time. This is next time." She smiled as her hand found its goal, the smile deepening at his immediate, very obvious reaction.

"I have a feeling I'm going to like being married to you," Rob growled, shifting to pin her soft body beneath his hard one.

"Of course you are," she answered breathlessly. "What's not to like?"

THIS JULY, HARLEQUIN OFFERS YOU
THE PERFECT SUMMER READ!

Sunsational

EMMA DARCY
EMMA GOLDRICK
PENNY JORDAN
CAROLE MORTIMER

From top authors of Harlequin Presents comes
HARLEQUIN SUNSATIONAL, a four-stories-in-one
book with 768 pages of romantic reading.

Written by such prolific Harlequin authors as Emma Darcy,
Emma Goldrick, Penny Jordan and Carole Mortimer,
HARLEQUIN SUNSATIONAL is the perfect summer
companion to take along to the beach, cottage, on your
dream destination or just for reading at home in the warm
sunshine!

Don't miss this unique reading opportunity.

Available wherever Harlequin books are sold.

Take 4 bestselling love stories FREE

Plus get a FREE surprise gift!

Special Limited-time Offer

Mail to
Harlequin Reader Service®
3010 Walden Avenue
P.O. Box 1867
Buffalo, N.Y. 14269-1867

YES! Please send me 4 free Harlequin Temptation® novels and my free surprise gift. Then send me 4 brand-new novels every month, which I will receive months before they appear in bookstores. Bill me at the low price of $2.64 each—a savings of 31¢ apiece off cover prices. There are no shipping, handling or other hidden costs. I understand that accepting the books and gift places me under no obligation ever to buy any books. I can always return a shipment and cancel at any time. Even if I never buy another book from Harlequin, the 4 free books and the surprise gift are mine to keep forever.

142 BPA AC9N

Name   (PLEASE PRINT)

Address   Apt. No.

City   State   Zip

This offer is limited to one order per household and not valid to present Harlequin Temptation® subscribers. Terms and prices are subject to change. Sales tax applicable in N.Y.

TEMP-BPA20R

© 1990 Harlequin Enterprises Limited

Back by Popular Demand

Janet Dailey
Americana

A romantic tour of America through fifty favorite Harlequin Presents, each set in a different state researched by Janet and her husband, Bill. A journey of a lifetime in one cherished collection.

In August, don't miss the exciting states featured in:

Title #13 — ILLINOIS
The Lyon's Share

#14 — INDIANA
The Indy Man

Available wherever
Harlequin books are sold.

JD-AUG